Kid Smarts

Wistful Hearts

KC Hart

To Mrs. Lucille
That day at church when you hugged me and told me you were proud
of me will always be one of the most special memories I will have

Books By KC Hart

A Christmas Blaze

Fresh Starts and Small Town Hearts

Business Smarts and Reckless Hearts

Car Smarts and Bashful Hearts

People Smarts and Wounded Hearts

Kid Smarts and Wistful Hearts

Family Smarts and Runaway Hearts

Elsie: Prairie Roses Collection

Moonlight, Murder and Small Town Secrets

Music, Murder and Small Town Romance

Memories. Murder and Small Town Money

Merry Murder and Small Town Santas

Medicine Murder and Small Town Scandal

Marriage, Murder & Small Town Schemes

Mistaken Murder & Small Town Status

Mistletoe, Murder & Small Town Scoundrels

Join KC's newsletter and receive a free ebook of Music Smarts and Humble Hearts

Chapter One

"You're ugly." Molly Lewis glared at her big brother, her four-year-old chin firm with stubborn indignation.

"Dad." Scout Lewis shouted through the living room toward the kitchen as he threw down his little sister's tennis shoe. No answer. "You can go to school barefoot, for all I care." He stomped into the bathroom and slammed the door, listening as the expected screams and sobs of his little sister filled the house.

"Scout." Drake Lewis's voice called over Molly's continued shrieks, almost vibrating the bathroom door. "What's wrong with your sister?"

Scout kept putting the toothpaste on his brush, ignoring the cacophony of noise beyond the sanctity of the locked door. Gracie always managed to disappear when Molly needed something done. Today Scout was following her example.

"What's the matter, squirt?" Drake walked into the living room, wiping his damp hands on a kitchen towel. "You sound like somebody chopped off your big toe." He stepped over to where his youngest daughter continued to sob, her unruly mass of tight blond curls sticking out in every direction, so much like her mother's that it made Drake's heart ache. "Hey, hey, hey." He sat down on the couch and pulled the four-year-old into his lap. "All that cat-a-walling's not helping anything. Take a breath and tell me what's going on."

"Scout said I was a baby." Molly wiped the back of her hand across her drippy nose. She looked up at her daddy with deep blue eyes fringed with surprisingly dark lashes. "He said I needed baby shoes that babies could put on until I could learn to tie my own."

Drake picked up the tail of his t-shirt and wiped his youngest child's snotty nose. It had started running Saturday evening after the kids came back from his momma's. He had heard his daughter coughing several times throughout the night. He laid his hand on her forehead. "You're a little warm." He leaned over and picked up her shoe. He was off from the hardware store today since he worked Saturday, but he was supposed to look at the plumbing over at a house in the garden district. Maybe Momma could watch her today. He would give Molly some Tylenol with breakfast.

Molly let out a barking cough as he slipped on her shoe and tied the laces. No, she needed to go to the clinic. He would have to take her in, then do the plumbing job later. "How does skipping school sound today? You can hang out with me then go see Mawmaw after while." The crying that sounded like the child was going through irreparable emotional damage stopped so suddenly that the quiet pounded in Drake's ears.

"Good," she said. I don't like school. I'm smart without it. Mawmaw says so."

"Well, you have to learn to read. How are you going to come work at the hardware store with me if you don't learn to read?" He stood, hoisting the child up on his hip. "Where's your brother and sister? We need to eat breakfast and hit the road, or they're going to be late for school again."

"Scout's in the bathroom, and Gracie went outside to check on Rambler."

Drake shook his head as he walked over to the window and looked out at the frost and mist on the icy cold February ground. Gracie, his seven-year-old, squatted barefoot in the grass in her flannel nightgown, looking under his truck. He dropped Molly down to the floor and stepped toward his front door. "Go get in your chair and pick out which biscuit you want."

He opened his front door, and freezing winter air gushed into the living room. "Gracie Nell Lewis, get in this house right now." His voice bellowed across the yard loud enough to wake the neighbors. It didn't matter. Momma's house was up the hill. Quinn, his little brother, lived in the double-wide across the road, and his older brother Hank lived on his other side. They were used to his yelling, although Hank was never home to hear it.

Gracie stood and looked over her shoulder at her father, not the least bit worried by his fierce tone. She slowly moped back to the front porch, the frosty ground crunching under her feet. Rambler, Quinn's mutt of the "Heinz 57" variety, had been the topic of a heated discussion last night before bedtime. When Quinn was home from offshore, the dog stayed across the road where he belonged, but Quinn, being Quinn, didn't bother with what happened to the animal while he was out on his seven day hitch. Drake had come in to tell the girls goodnight and found the ancient dog piled up in the bed with Gracie, fleas and all.

"Daddy, he'll freeze tonight. I promised Uncle Quinn I'd take care of Rambler when he was gone. He gave me five dollars to put food in his bowl every day."

"I don't care if he gave you a gold monkey. That old dog is

not sleeping in your bed. He can go sleep in Mawmaw's shed with Poochie and be just fine."

"But he is my responsibility, Dad." Gracie's eyes had teared up as she wrapped her arms around the slobbery old hound. "He needs me."

Quinn Lewis, I'm going to skin you alive. "He's not your responsibility. He's Uncle Quinn's." He reached down and pulled the dog from the bed onto the floor. "Besides, Poochie needs Rambler to snuggle to tonight to keep her warm."

"Mawmaw said Poochie needs to stay away from Rambler or some baby Poochie's will be showing up soon."

"Don't you worry about Poochie and Rambler." Drake kissed his middle child, her sandy brown hair falling in her eyes, so much like his own had been at that age. "Mawmaw and Uncle Quinn need to learn how to take care of their dog's business, so they won't have those problems."

He reached down and put his hand on Gracie's back, hustling her into the living room. How come she could practically run around buck naked in the dead of winter and never get a sniffle while Molly seemed to be sick every time he turned around? "You're as cold as a frog, Gracie, and you smell like a dog. Go wash up. We're going to be late again."

Drake nudged his middle daughter in the direction of the bathroom and stepped into the hallway to check on Scout. It wasn't like him to not be in the thick of things, ordering his sisters around, and trying to take on the role of man of the house. His son's bedroom door was cracked open, and Drake stuck his head in the door, but stopped at what he saw. Scout, his coat on, his schoolbag on his back, was kneeling by his bed, his eyes closed.

"God, I'm doing what I can to help Daddy, but sometimes I'm not enough."

Drake's eyes filled with compassion as his son's prayer filled his heart.

"Daddy is trying, but sometimes he gets mad because things don't go right. So, God, I was wondering if you could bring Daddy a wife. He tries to act like he doesn't need one, but I can tell he does. I figured if I could tell, then, God, you can tell too. That's all I'm asking for, God." Scout pulled his hands down from where he had them folded in prayer but pushed them back up. "And I'm really sorry for being mean to Molly this morning, but you know she started it. Amen."

Esther pulled her thick mane of caramel colored curls back in a loose ponytail at the nape of her neck. The sudden drop in temperature from the sixties last week to the thirties over the weekend had brought in a flood of the routine asthmatics, along with several more kids with signs of respiratory infections. A few children had tested positive for strep, but thankfully they hadn't seen any patients testing positive for influenza.

She washed her hands as she stared into the bathroom mirror. Her lips were still a little chapped from being out in the wind over the weekend helping her twin brother Barlow wrap their pipes. She tugged down the gray scrub top over her middle and tossed the damp paper towels in the trash. The suit was getting a little snug, but it was still okay to wear. She hadn't gotten on the scales lately, but she'd put on several pounds over the past three months. She was built just like her mother and most of the women in her family, short with plenty of curves. The extra pounds were what Granny referred to as her winter coat. She would probably drop them again when spring arrived, and she started playing softball with the ladies at the church. Then again, she was turning thirty this year. This fuller look might be her new normal. If it was, that would be okay, too.

"Esther, the Lewis kid is in room four," Sandy, the med tech, said as they stepped up to the nurse's desk.

"Which one?" Esther looked down at the never-ending flow of charts. Getting off at four this afternoon to go visit her grandparents was not going to happen.

"The wild one." Sandy rolled her eyes and slid the chart in front of Esther. "I can see if Dianne will take her, but you know the mood she's in today."

"No, that's fine." Esther took the chart from the med tech's hand. "I'll see her. Let's not ruffle Dianne's feathers if we don't have to."

Esther opened the chart as she stepped to the exam room door. Molly Lewis was a frequent flyer and had developed a reputation for being hard to handle. She and Dianne, the other nurse practitioner, took turns seeing the child, and technically today was Dianne's day. A young patient had already vomited on Diane first thing this morning, however, and Esther decided that it would be better for the entire staff if she just saw the child.

A barking cough sounded on the other side of the door as Esther placed her hand on the door handle. That didn't sound good. "Is there a puppy loose in here?" She stepped into the room and looked behind the trash can, then walked over and looked on the other side of the exam table. "I know I heard barking in here. Molly Lewis, did you bring a puppy into this clinic?"

"No." Molly's forehead wrinkled with a determine frown. "That was me, and I'm not a dog."

"You?" Esther put her hands on her hips and looked down at the spunky little blond. She had obviously picked out her own attire this morning. Lime green sweatpants stuck out from under a flouncy red dress with puffy sleeves and a lacy collar. She had tucked one leg of her sweats into her worn cowboy boots and stretched the other one around the top of it. "Are you sure you don't have a puppy under the tail of that pretty red dress?" She slipped her stethoscope from the pocket of her scrubs and inched closer to the child. Molly Lewis was a kicker, and it paid to move in slowly.

"I told you no." The child coughed again, and Esther looked over at Drake, sitting in the nearby chair. That was another reason she didn't mind seeing the tenacious child, the real reason, actually. Drake Lewis was easy on the eye. She had known Drake, Quinn, and Hank ever since her parents had moved to Carson's Bayou when she was a kid in junior high. She'd had a crush on him almost as long.

"She's had a snotty nose for a few days, but that coughing, and the fever started last night." Drake's deep somber voice filled the little exam room, and he stood up by the table where Molly sat. "Since she gets the croup so easily, I figured I'd better bring her on in."

"You did the right thing." Esther put the stethoscope in her ears and leaned in closer. "Okay, Molly, it's time for me to take a listen."

"No." Molly's eyes shot daggers at Esther, and she leaned over on Drake, away from Esther. "I don't like you, and you're not touching me." She pulled her knee in and kicked out, but Esther swerved, dodging the kick.

"Alright, Molly Paige." Drake eased his daughter up straight. "You remember what we talked about on the way here? If you cooperate, I'll get you a doughnut from the coffee shop when we're done. If you show out and act like you don't have any raisings, we're going straight home."

"Can I get a doughnut with chocolate on top and one with pink on top?" Molly cut her eyes up at her father and coughed again, right on cue.

Esther watched the child, amazed at how she played

Drake Lewis, one of the toughest men in the parish, like he was a bass fiddle. Back in high school Drake had been the captain of the football team and had often been involved in pranks played on rival schools. When she and Barlow had been away at college, Drake had gotten a reputation for being wild; drinking and partying every weekend. Back then, Barlow or the rest of her conservative family would never have allowed her to go out with Drake Lewis or any of the Lewis boys. Not that he had ever given her a second glance. He hadn't.

Then, ten years ago, Esther had come home for Christmas break during her sophomore year of college. She liked to have fallen off her seat in the choir when Paige Floyd came walking through the back doors of the church with Drake on her arm. Before Esther went back to school two weeks later, Drake had given his life to Christ. She had gone back to college, and the next thing she heard, the two had gotten married. Drake's wild partying ways had come to a stop.

"Yes, I'll get you whatever you want. Just let Miss Esther listen to your chest." Drake looked down at his daughter, his eyebrows raised. "Do we have a deal?"

"I'll do it," the little girl said, poking her lips out, "but I still don't like her. I think she's fat and ugly too."

Chapter Two

Esther rubbed her fingertips over her eyes. It had been a long day. All she wanted to do was soak in a tub, eat a bowl of ice cream, then curl up with a good book. She grabbed a basket from the stack by the automatic doors at the front of the grocery store. It was already after six, and cooking supper was not in the plans for tonight. The ice cream and cold cereal, her top two evening meal choices after killer days like today, were both gone. It was either run in here or starve until in the morning.

She nodded to one of the cashiers checking out an elderly lady with an enormous bag of cat food. She strode to the back of the store, an orchestra version of an old Elton John song playing overhead. Humming along, she passed the canned goods and rice and pasta aisles. *I need to grab a Mountain Dew on the way out.*

Granny had been sympathetic when Esther called and told her she couldn't come by this afternoon. One day she planned on being the kind of grandmother her granny was, if that day ever came. *Like that's going to happen. First, I have to find a decent guy, get married, actually have a kid and raise it to have children of his or her own. None of those things seem to be in my fore-seeable future.*

Guys asked her out, and she went out on the occasional date, but so far, no one had measured up to her idea of the marrying type of man. Drake Lewis, standing at the check-out desk earlier today with his daughter riding on his hip, drifted into her head. Drake was rough around the edges, probably always would be, but seeing the man taking care of his daughter the way he did made her heart do an extra beat.

She grabbed the ice cream and a half gallon of milk from the cold section before heading toward the breakfast aisle. No need to even go there. Drake Lewis was so wrapped up in his kids that he didn't seem to notice any of the women around him. They noticed him though. That was for sure.

"That man knows how to fill out them jeans," Sandy had whispered as she, and most of the other women in the back of the clinic, watched him walk down the hallway to check out this morning. Of course, Esther had been looking right along with them. She had been looking since she was thirteen years old.

"I don't like that kind."

The familiar voice of Molly Lewis trumpeted from around the end cap of the breakfast aisle, almost like Esther had conjured the girl up by daydreaming about her father. Esther rounded the corner and stared.

"Molly." Scout, the older brother barked at his sister in a shushed tone. "You picked last time. You know it's Gracie's turn to pick out the cereal."

Esther looked past the children, searching for their father, but he was nowhere in sight. Should she step in and stop the ensuing disaster? *Would he want me meddling in his business?* Every time she had seen him and the children, he was always so attentive to them. He would probably appreciate her intervention. She took a step toward the arguing kids, her hands on her hips.

"We're not getting Fruity Pebbles," Gracie, the middle daughter yelled, grabbing the enormous off brand bag of cereal from Molly. Molly's hands clutched the plastic in a death grip, jerking the cereal bag backwards."

"Hey kids," Esther hurried toward them, but the children ignored her.

"Molly. Let go." Scout grabbed another corner of the bag, ripping it apart, sending an explosion of beautiful fruity colors up into the air, showering down all over the children... and Esther.

"Oh." Molly's eyes and mouth formed a perfect circle. "Look what you did, Scout," she said, watching the sugary smelling dust from the cereal float down all around them. "Daddy's gonna get you good."

Esther closed her eyes then opened them again. Fruity Pebbles littered the children's hair and clothing. She rolled her eyes up and pulled a piece of orange colored rice from one of her curls. "Where's your father?" Esther stepped forward, the cereal crunching under her feet, and took the empty ripped bag from Scouts hand. "He needs to get someone to clean this up."

"It wasn't my fault, Molly, and you know it." Scout frowned down at his little sister, then looked up at Esther. "Daddy told Gracie to get the cereal today, not Molly."

"I'll let your father sort that out later," Esther said, looking from Scout to Gracie who was staring at the mess all around them. "Where is he, anyway?"

"I step away for three seconds." Drake's voice boomed behind Esther, and she turned around. "Three seconds, and y'all destroy the place," he said, his voice not as loud. His narrowed eyes glared at his children, then the floor scattered with the multi-colored cereal. He looked at Esther and rolled his eyes. "All I did was step around the corner to grab some toilet paper, and... Molly, stop that."

Esther turned to where Drake was looking. No wonder the girl got away with so much. She shook her head and tried to force down the laughter bubbling up inside her. Molly, crouched down on all fours, was raking the cereal up in a pile and cramming fistfuls in her mouth, like she hadn't eaten in days. Esther's laughter echoed down the aisle, and Molly looked up, her cheeks stuffed with cereal. "I'm hungry and don't like Cheerios no more," she said, as if it was perfectly normal to eat cereal off the floor.

"You want a kid?" Drake stepped past Esther and scooped up Molly. "Momma says I'm just reaping what I sowed with this one, and she's probably right."

"Seems like I remember you going to the principal's office a couple of times for starting food fights in the cafeteria back in the day."

"Hey now." Fruity Pebbles crunched as Drake turned, taking in the mess, holding Molly like a sack of potatoes. "I didn't start any of those fights, I just really enjoyed them once they got going." He looked down into the wild mess of blond curls on his daughter's head. "It'll take all night to get this stuff out of your hair."

"Dad." Gracie tugged at Drake's leg. "I'm hungry. Are we about done? Can I get Honey Nut Cheerios?"

"Not yet." Drake looked at the disaster his children made of the cereal aisle. "We have to help clean this up, or they may ban us from the grocery store. If that happens, how will we get our food?" He reached down and tussled Gracie's hair. "We'll grab your cereal before we leave. Scout." Drake shifted Molly who continued to hang loosely on his one arm, listening to how her daddy was reacting to their little fiasco. "Go see if you can find a store worker and a broom."

Esther looked at Scout's drooping shoulders, Gracie's

tired face, and Molly, licking the fruity pebbles stuck on her arm. "Take your kids on home, Drake. I'll let the manager know what happened and help get this cleaned up."

"I can't ask you to do that, Esther. These three know that when you make a mess you have to stay and clean it up."

Esther smiled up at Drake. He reached out and pulled a flake of red cereal from one of her curls. "I'll go with Scout to find a clerk," she said, putting her hand on the boy's shoulder. "How about that?"

"Kids, tell Miss Esther thank you for the help." Drake flipped Molly into an upright position and set her on her feet. "Don't eat any more of that cereal off the floor, girl, or I'll skin you alive," he said, his voice firm. "As easy as you get sick, you'll catch a bug and be back at the clinic tomorrow."

"Thank you, Miss Esther," Scout said stepping closer to where Esther stood.

"Thank you," Molly and Gracie mumbled in unison.

"Here." Drake reached over and took the basket holding the milk and ice cream from Esther's hands. "I'll hold that for you until you get back."

Esther took Scout's hand as they started to the front of the store.

"What did y'all do with our buggy?" Drake asked. "I promise, girls, you two are going to be the death of me yet."

Esther listened to Drake's voice behind her as she and Scout walked away. She smiled, the fatigue weighing her down from a few minutes ago drifting away.

"Miss Esther."

"Hmm?" Esther looked down at Scout, his hand still in hers. "Does my hair look as silly as yours?"

"It has cereal in it, if that's what you mean," Scout said, smiling up at Esther, showing the gap between his two front teeth. "Do you want to come eat supper with Daddy one night?"

"What?" Esther stopped and stared down at the little boy.

"Can you come to our house and eat supper?" Scout peered up at Esther, waiting for an answer.

"I think you had better clear it with your daddy before you invite someone over for supper, don't you?"

"If Daddy says it's okay, will you come to supper one night?"

Esther's lips stretched into a smile. *He's a strong-willed little thing. Probably has to be to live with those little sisters.* "If your daddy ever decides to invite me to supper, I'll accept. Now come on. We have to get somebody to help with that mess."

They found a checker who didn't have any customers, and Esther informed him that they needed help. The teenaged checker told the next cashier to notify the manager about the spill. He followed Esther and Scout back to the cereal aisle.

At the edge of the spill, Gracie and Molly stood back to back, arms crossed over their chests like a couple of angry statues. Drake was working in a circle pushing the cereal into a pile with the side of his cowboy boot. The store manager showed up from the other end of the aisle with a push broom and a super-sized dustpan as Esther, Scout, and the teen walked up.

"We'll clean this up, Mr. Lewis," the man said, handing his broom and dustpan to the teen beside Esther. "You go on with your shopping."

"I'm really sorry about this," Drake said to the manager. He took the hands of both the girls. "Now, you two come show me where you hid my buggy."

"I can take my basket back now," Esther said, stepping in line with Drake and the children as they left the cereal aisle.

"Oh." Drake released Gracie's hand and slid the basket off his arm. "Here you go. I'm sorry we slowed you up, and sorry for the cereal they spilled on you."

"It's no problem." Esther took the basket from Drake's

hand, her fingers brushing against his. "It was kind of enter-taining."

"Dad." Scout, who had been trailing silently behind his father and sisters, stepped around Molly and tugged on Drake's leg. "I invited Miss Esther to come eat with us on Valentine's Day and she said she would."

Esther's eyes shot down to Scout, her eyebrows raised. "Now, Scout, that's not exactly what I said."

"Daddy." Scout didn't look at Esther but continued to stare up at his father. "We need to thank her for helping us, don't we?"

"Yes." Drake looked from his son over to Esther, his lips pushed up into a polite smile. "You're right, Scout. Esther, do you want to come out to the house Friday evening for supper?"

"Well, I..." Heat crept up Esther's neck.

"Please," Scout pleaded. "We will all be good, even Molly. I promise."

Esther looked at the four faces, all waiting for an answer. Drake continued with his polite smile. Gracie looked mildly curious. Molly's lips pushed down into a defiant frown. Esther pulled in a breath of air and blew it out. In her daydreams, this was not how Drake Lewis asked her out on their first date. Still, it was a date... sort of. "I guess I can come."

"She said yes, Daddy." Scout beamed up at Drake. "That's good, huh?"

"That's good." Drake nodded, his smile still polite. "How does six sound?"

"That sounds great." Esther grinned. *Don't look like you just won the lottery. He's being nice because his son cornered him in to asking you.* "I'll see you Friday."

Chapter Three

"Yes, she is a very nice lady." Drake lifted Gracie from the backseat of his double-cab truck onto the ground in their front yard. He grabbed the lightest grocery bag full of cereal and toilet paper and handed it down to his son's waiting arms. "The point I'm making is, you know you are supposed to ask me before inviting anybody over to the house like that."

"I thought that was only with my friends," Scout said. He took the bag from his father's hands and stepped back. Drake lifted Molly from the back and set her down beside Scout. "I thought asking adults would be okay since you didn't have to take care of them, or nothing like you have to do when Colby spends the night."

Drake grabbed the rest of the grocery bags and shut the truck door with his hip. "Molly, leave that dog alone." Rambler licked the sugary coating of cereal dust from the youngest daughter's arm and nudged his nose into her curly head. "Shoo, Rambler," Drake yelled. The dog ignored Drake and nuzzled against Molly. "Scout, get that dog off your sister." Molly laid her head over on the dog's back, ignoring her father.

Scout grabbed Molly's shirt and pulled her off the dog, shoving her toward Gracie, who was already walking toward the front door. "Go on, Rambler, Scout said. "Gracie will feed you in a minute." The family started across the mostly dirt covered yard with the occasional patch of grass sticking up among the mud puddles and brick hard ground. "I'll help you cook supper for her, Dad. We can have beans and weenies."

"We'll see, son." Drake set down the bags in his right hand and sorted through the keys in his fingers. He pulled open the screen and stuck the key in the front door, shoving it open with his boot while holding the screen open with his hip. He bent down and picked up the groceries as the children trailed in. A gust of winter wind, not extremely cold but still a little chilly, whirled around them.

"I want a snack," Molly said, watching Drake walk in and slam the door with his foot. The winter temperature had climbed up from the thirties and forties last week to the sixties and seventies this week, typical for Louisiana. If it weren't for the occasional wind, it would seem like spring had arrived in February. Molly sat on the floor and started pulling off her tennis shoes and socks. "I want a snack," she said again to the room in general, "then I'm going outside."

"You've got to have a bath." Drake stepped over his daughter and headed toward the kitchen. "All three of you are a sticky mess." He dumped the grocery bags on the kitchen table where the family ate all of their meals and walked back to the living room. "Gracie, you and Scout start putting up the refrigerator food while I run some bathwater. Make sure you don't leave that bacon out. It costs an arm and a leg." He looked down at Molly, standing near the front door. "You come with me. We're liable to clog up the drain, washing all that mess from your hair."

"Dad." Gracie whined, standing up from where she had flopped onto the couch. "I need to feed Rambler first. He's hungry. Can't Scout do the groceries?"

"Help your brother," Drake barked. "Uncle Quinn should be in today. That dog won't starve before he can feed it."

Drake stepped into the compact bathroom and pulled back the shower curtain decorated with Disney princesses and turned on the bath water. He stuck the rubber stopper in the drain and looked back at Molly, tugging her t-shirt over her head. The child really was rotten, no doubt about it. If she didn't have Paige's sky-blue eyes or that crazy curly blond hair of her mother's, or even that thing she did when she was trying to make you laugh, he could probably discipline her better. Every time he looked at the child, she reminded him of his wife. The wife who had sacrificed everything to make him happy. Now, he was here raising their kids, and she was gone.

He reached over and pulled the t-shirt over Molly's head, shaking a shower of Fruity Pebbles from her hair onto the Paw Patrol bathmat under her feet. "Don't eat those," he said, scooping up his daughter as she knelt and started gathering up the cereal and shoving it in her mouth. He plopped her in the tub, and she leaned back and rolled over, stretching out like she was in an Olympic sized pool. He turned off the faucets and tossed a washcloth in the water. "Start scrubbing."

What was he going to do about tomorrow night? He had known Esther forever. In junior high and high school, she would sometimes come with Barlow over to their house. Drake's family moved from the house in town, after his father died his seventh grade year. Barlow had put an end to her tagging along with him later when they were in high school. It was not because he minded her hanging out with him and Drake. It was Quinn. He was a year younger but much too experienced for his sixteen years, and started noticing Esther a little too much for Barlow's liking. Drake couldn't see Esther ever giving Quinn a second glance, even though he had a reputation for charming the legs off a snake.

Drake had not been an angel back then, but his wildness ran more along the lines of driving too fast and somehow always finding an underdog that needed taking up for. Then the twins moved off to college, and he met Paige.

"I'm not a wild girl like the ones you hang out with." Paige had said to Quinn all those years ago in front of the drugstore. "I think you would get bored with me, or I would have to slap you silly. Either way, there's no need for us to go out."

"How about me?" Drake had heard the words coming out of his mouth that day, but had not been able to stop them.

"Now you, Drake Lewis." Paige smiled that slow smile that had captured his heart. "You might do."

After that day, his life had never been the same. By that time, he had been a weekend drinker, not because he particularly cared about the alcohol, but why not? There wasn't a lot else to do in Carson's Bayou after watching the high school football game. His momma didn't care as long as he didn't bring any trouble to her door. But Paige, Paige cared. For Paige, he gave it all up. For Paige, he started attending church.

"Daddy, watch." Molly splashed water onto Drake's leg as he sat on the edge of the tub. "I can blow bubbles."

"You sound like a motorboat." Drake got on his knees beside the tub and squirted strawberry shampoo into his palm. "Flip over and lean back. We've got to work on that rat's nest."

"I wish I had hair like Gracie and Scout and you." Molly leaned her head back and rested it in one of Drake's hands. He rubbed the shampoo into the mass of curls, then poured water over the yellow locks with a cup from the tub. "Mine is too messy," she said, opening her eyes and staring up at her father.

"I love your hair." Drake looked down at the child's face, her eyes narrowed with concern. "You have hair like your mother, and that makes you all the more special."

"And I look like Momma, and she was beautiful." Molly's serious face contemplated what her daddy had told her so many times in her young life. "I'm beautiful too, huh?"

"Yes, you are." Drake dumped another cup of water on the child's hair, careful to keep it from her eyes. "But remember that when you act ugly and make God unhappy, it doesn't matter what you look like."

"Being good is hard."

"I know." Drake raised his daughter to a sitting position and lifted himself from the side of the tub. "But you shouldn't have kicked at Miss Esther at the doctor's office. You know she was trying to help you." Drake pulled the towel from the bar and wrapped it around his daughter's shoulders as she stood.

"She is always poking me when I see her. If she can poke me, then I can kick her." Molly stood still as Drake lifted her from the bathwater and set her on the floor. "Mawmaw says you don't start nothing, but you don't have to take nothing either."

"I'm going to have to have a talk with Mawmaw." Drake stepped toward the door. "Miss Esther is coming to the house tomorrow evening for dinner. I expect you to act as pretty as you look. Do you understand?"

"If she don't poke me, I won't mess with her." The child's lips stuck out in a thin line as a loose cough rose from her chest. "Rules are rules."

"Dad. I dropped my milk." Gracie's voice called from the kitchen. "I'm gonna let Rambler in to lick it up."

"You stay in this bathroom while I grab your pajamas and underwear." Drake opened the bathroom door, then looked back at the tub full of water littered with soap bubbles and breakfast cereal. He stepped back to the tub and pulled the plug from the drain. Best to remove the temptation of another swim from his headstrong daughter.

A gust of air rushed past him as he hurried to the girls' room to grab Molly's night clothes. Gracie must have opened the front door. He stepped into the bedroom and pulled open a dresser drawer. Molly didn't need to catch a chill, but if he left her in the bathroom alone too long, she would run through the house naked as a jaybird. "Gracie, don't let that dog in the kitchen," he called over his shoulder. He pulled out a wrinkled zip up fleece onesie and underwear from the drawer stuffed with wadded up clothes. Who had time to fold?

"Dad." Scout called from somewhere in the house, his voice tense.

"I'll be right there, son." Drake stepped across the hall and threw the clothes into the bathroom toward his four-year-old. "Molly Paige. What have I told you about the powder?" He looked at his daughter, every inch of her looking like she had been rolled in powdered sugar.

"Dad!" Scout's yell was definitely worried.

"Don't move." Drake gave Molly a stern frown as he shut the bathroom door and hurried to the kitchen. Scout stood in front of the open refrigerator holding a carton of eggs. Gracie had one end of the package of bacon in her hands playing tug of war with Rambler, holding the other end of the package in his mouth. Milk puddled around the wooden floor at their feet.

"He pulled it off the table," Gracie said, fear in her voice. "I didn't give it to him, Daddy, I promise."

Drake stepped over and took the package from his daughter's hands, jerking it from the dog's mouth. He tossed the mangled package in the sink and reached under the table where the dog had retreated. "I know, honey, but you know I don't like that dog in the house."

"Mawmaw and Uncle Quinn let him in their house, and Mawmaw lets him in here when you are at work."

Drake grabbed Rambler by the collar and drug him to the front door. He reached for the knob, but the door flew open before he touched it.

"Hello. Big Brother. You aren't trying to steal my dog, now, are you?" Quinn Lewis stepped into the living room in dark-washed jeans, cowboy boots, and a tight black t-shirt.

"Uncle Quinn." Molly, wearing nothing but her thick layer of powder, flew across the room and wrapped her arms around Quinn's legs. "We're so glad you're home. Aren't we, Daddy?"

Drake stepped around his brother and slid the dog out the front door. He turned and looked at his kids, all staring at his little brother like he hung the moon. "Yeah. Welcome home." Drake went to the bathroom and grabbed Molly's towel and clothes.

"I tried to sneak in Rambler like you said, Uncle Quinn, but Daddy caught me." Gracie's loud whisper carried down the hall, and Drake slowed his steps.

"Don't you worry about your daddy," Quinn said, his laughter filling the living room. "He's just an old grump. All of us will have some fun this weekend while he's at work. How does going mudding on the four-wheeler sound?"

"Molly had to go to the doctor with a chest cold." Drake stepped into the living room. "They don't need to get out and get wet in the middle of winter. I don't care if it is sixty degrees."

"Sure thing, Big Brother." Quinn winked at the kids and grinned at Drake. "You're the boss."

This has got to change. Drake looked around the room at the spilled milk, groceries spilling off the table, Molly's powder footprints tracked up the hall, and dog hair from one end of the room to the other. He slipped the clothes on Molly and went into the kitchen, leaving the children chatting away with Quinn on the couch. *Lord, I don't know how to fix this, but they deserve better. They need stability and consistency. Momma and Quinn do not need to be their only other role models. Help me figure out how to make this better.*

Chapter Four

"**A**re you sure that's what you want to wear?" Scout's brow furrowed as he looked at his dad. "You have that suit, you know."

"Son, this is fine." Drake looked down at his faded jeans and white t-shirt. He had gone to the extra trouble this morning of taking the shirt out of the drawer and hanging it up so it wouldn't be so wrinkled when he put it on this evening. What more did the kid expect? "That suit is for funerals. I'm not even sure it still fits."

"I think you look beautiful, Daddy," Gracie said, smiling up at Drake from her seat at the dining room table. "Can I help serve the spaghetti?"

"No, Gracie." Scout looked around their dining table set in the corner of the kitchen like he was a health inspector for a five-star restaurant. "This food is for Daddy and Miss Esther. We have to stay in our rooms and be quiet when she comes."

"I'm not staying in my room." Molly's lips stuck out in a pout. "I want brownies and ice cream too."

Drake shoved the tub of butter back in the fridge and

eyed his children. Scout was obviously playing matchmaker tonight, even though he'd explained that he and Miss Esther were only longtime friends. "Nobody has to stay anywhere, and Gracie, you can serve the rolls. We're all having brownies and ice cream for dessert. How about that?"

"Thank you, Daddy. I told Scout you would let us eat with you." Gracie turned her nose up at her brother and slid out of her chair. "I'm going to go put on my sparkly shoes. I'll be right back."

"Daddy." Scout rolled his eyes at his father. "I have it all planned out."

"Sorry, son." Drake walked over and tussled his son's sandy brown hair. "If Miss Esther wants to visit me, she has to visit with you and your sisters too. We're a package deal."

"Come on, Molly." Scout's shoulders sagged, and he stepped over and took his baby sister's hand. "Let's go get your shoes on. You better be good tonight. No kicking or saying bad words."

"Mawmaw and Uncle Quinn say shoot all the time. If they can say it, I can say it."

Drake listened as Scout led Molly down the hall to her and Gracie's room, trying to give her a lesson on morality. He looked at the dining room table set with the mismatched plates stacked in the corner. He stepped out to the back porch and brought in the wobbly cane back chair where he drank his coffee most mornings before he woke the kids. He scooted it in on the side where Molly sat. Scout would have to give up his normal seat for Esther tonight and sit by his little sister.

Oh well. He looked around their kitchen with the coloring sheets stuck to the refrigerator and the crayon marks on the lower half of the white sheetrock from the kids' younger days of creativity. He needed to scrub those off, but when was he supposed to find time for that? He dropped the kids off at school every morning on his way to the hardware store, and they rode the bus to his mother's every evening. After he finished at the store, he usually squeezed in one or two handyman jobs around town. On his day off, he was always working on his handyman side job. He needed the money. Scout would need braces in a few years, and every time he got a little cash put up in savings, something broke. Sunday was his only actual day off. Even then, Sunday afternoons always filled up with an overflow of things he hadn't gotten done through the week. *If it's good enough for us, it will have to be good enough for Esther.*

Knock, knock. Drake wiped his hands on a dishtowel and tossed it on the cabinet. "Here goes nothing." He ran his hands across the top of his short hair, just a shade darker than his two oldest children's, and stepped through the living room to the front door.

Drake opened the door, and the soft scent of coconut mixed with citrus tickled his nose. Esther Sartin smiled up at him from the doorway, and a timid current of excitement, one he had forgotten existed, ran through his gut. "Hey, Esther." He smiled and pulled the door open wide. "Come in if you can get in. We are about as informal as you can get around here."

Esther stepped through the door and slipped her white sweater from her shoulders. "Thank you for having me over, Drake. I know it wasn't exactly your idea, but I believe it will be fun to catch up. Don't you?"

Drake watched the sweater slip down Esther's shoulders, admiring her toned arms, not too skinny. He took in her curvy figure in the red dress with tiny white dots as she continued to talk. A woman needed curves, and Esther definitely had them in all the right places. Skinny women might be what everyone else thought were pretty, but not him. A woman needed to be a woman, not a stick.

"Drake?"

"Yeah, yeah. Sorry." Drake blinked his eyes and reached for Esther's sweater. "Come on in." *Where did all that come from? I haven't thought about that kind of thing in... years.*

"I said I hope Molly is feeling better." Esther smiled at Drake, a twinkle in her eyes. "I think I lost you there for a minute."

"Sorry. I was just thinking... well... you look nice. I normally only see you in the scrubs. Not that you don't look nice in the scrubs." Drake reached over and hung her sweater up on the peg as he shut the front door behind her. "You know what I mean."

"Yeah, I know what you mean." Esther's smile broadened, and her eyes roamed around the living room. "Something smells great."

"Spaghetti, rolls, and salad with brownies and ice cream for dessert, nothing fancy."

"I love spaghetti. That sounds perfect." Esther looked over to the hallway where the three kids stood, watching the adults with inquisitive expressions. "I was hoping we were all going to eat together tonight. Girls, I love those shoes." Her smile stretched wide as Gracie and Molly came over to where she and Drake still stood near the front door. She squatted down and examined Gracie's glittery gold Mary Jane's and Molly's red ones. "I had a pair just like yours, Gracie, when I was about your age, and I always wanted a red pair, too."

"Watch this," Molly said, dancing around on their hardwood floor. "I can tap dance in mine."

"I'm impressed. You dance like a fairy." Esther stood back up, and Drake put his hand on Molly's head, stopping her performance. Esther looked at Scout, standing a little behind the girls. "Thank you for inviting me, Scout. I wouldn't have had anywhere to go on Valentine's Day if you hadn't."

"Scout, if you grin any wider, you're gonna break your

face," Drake said, looking at his son. "Alright, kids. Go wash your hands. I'm gonna stick those rolls in the oven. Esther, you can have a seat if you want to."

"You want to see our room?" Molly tugged at Esther's hand.

"Molly." Drake put on his stern face and looked down at his daughter. "Leave Miss Esther alone and go wash your hands. She's been working all day, and I'm sure she's ready to sit down."

"No, I'm fine." Esther smiled at Drake, then looked at the kid's expectant faces. "If it's alright with your dad, you go wash your hands, and when you're done, you can show me your rooms."

The three children's faces turned in unison to Drake. "That's fine by me. Just don't open any drawers or check in the closets."

"Yeah." Molly turned big round eyes back to Esther. "Cause we shoved them full of junk when we cleaned up a while ago, and they're trashier than a possum eating out of a dumpster."

Drake looked at Esther and shrugged his shoulders. "She's right. Enter at your own risk."

"I'm sure I can handle it," Esther said, winking at Drake. "You forget, I went into your bedroom a few times as a kid. I have a feeling that little apple doesn't fall far from the tree."

ESTHER TOOK another bite of the vanilla ice cream, making sure to get some brownie on her spoon. She sat on the love seat with Gracie beside her, and Drake and Molly sat across from them on the couch. Scout finished playing "Fleur de

Lis" on the old piano against the far wall and turned, waiting for her reaction.

"Scout." Esther set the spoon back in the bowl. "That was absolutely beautiful. You play so well."

"Thank you." Scout's face beamed. "Mrs. Sarah says I'm one of her best students."

"I can see why." Esther watched the boy walk over and squeeze in on the other side of his dad on the couch. "Most kids your age are playing Twinkle, Twinkle Little Star." She picked up the spoon and took another bite of ice cream and brownie. The child really had a gift. Hopefully, Drake would make sure he continued to receive the lessons to help it flourish.

"You want to see me dance again?" Molly set her empty ice cream bowl on the coffee table as she stood up. "One day I'm going to take ballet and get a tutu."

"Alright." Drake sat forward on the couch and scooped up his daughter. "No more performances tonight. It is way past your bedtimes."

Esther smiled as moans sounded from all three kids. "I sure have enjoyed this." She took Gracie's empty bowl as the child dragged herself from the seat. "That is some of the best spaghetti I've ever had."

"Daddy has a secret ingredient," Gracie said, looking at Esther, ice cream smeared across her upper lip.

"Whatever it is, it's great." Esther watched as Drake herded the children toward the hall. "There's coffee in the pot and mugs on the counter. I'll be right back."

Esther stood and gathered everyone's dessert bowls, then toted them into the kitchen. She ran some water in the sink and started washing up the dishes, listening to the children chatter with their father on the other side of the hall. She had been worried that Molly would act out tonight, not wanting her in their home, but she had been wrong. When they went to the girls' room before dinner, Molly showed her a ratty old stuffed monkey and asked her to check her chest. "Monkey Baby gets sick every time I do. I have to poke on him like you poke on me."

"Does Monkey Baby ever kick you like you try to kick me?" Esther asked, holding the little animal up to her ear, pretending to listen to him breathe.

"No. He's a good baby." Molly had reached up and touched one of Esther's curls hanging over her shoulder. "Your hair is curly like mine, huh?"

"Yes, except mine is the color of caramel and yours is the color of butter."

"Which is prettier?" Molly scooted up closer, almost getting into Esther's lap.

"I think butter." Esther reached over and touched one of Molly's curls. "What do you think?"

"I think butter too." Molly took the stuffed animal from Esther's hands. "I'm not going to try to kick you anymore when I come to your doctor place." She looked up at Esther. "Sometimes I'm a stubborn mule."

"You don't have to do that," Drake said, walking into the kitchen. "I was going to do that after you left."

Esther looked over her shoulder and smiled. "I don't mind." She lifted the last plate from the water and dipped it into the rinse water. "Getting to eat someone else's cooking has been great. I certainly don't mind helping with the clean-up. If you will put the leftovers in whatever you want them in so I can wash the pots, we will have this knocked out."

"Only if you agree to drink coffee when we're done."

"I'm in no hurry." Esther put the plate in the drainer with the rest of the dishes. "I would love to sit for a while and have coffee."

Chapter Five

Drake dried his hands on a dish towel and watched Esther pour her coffee. *Why was I so against this?* If Scout had not made it nearly impossible to get out of asking Esther over without seeming incredibly rude, this night would have never happened. She stood a few feet away, her hair falling in golden brown ripples down her back. He smiled. *This is nice. She made herself at home and hasn't really felt like company at all.*

"Do you have creamer?" Esther turned, holding a coffee mug with the hardware store's logo on the side. "I like coffee but can't handle it black."

"I have sugar and half and half." Drake took a step back, giving Esther room to turn around in the small corner. "Will that do? I drink coffee by the gallons, but only black. Momma uses the half and half."

"That will be perfect." She picked up a second mug with a faded John Deere logo on the side and handed it to Drake. "I'll doctor mine up while you pour yourself a cup."

Esther scooted past Drake, and he breathed in the coconut and citrus scent again. His fingers brushed against hers as he took the mug, and a tiny ripple ran up his arm. She opened the fridge, and he busied himself with the coffee. *She smells good. That's all.*

"If you don't mind, I'm going to get another brownie," Esther said, pulling a paper towel off the roll sitting on the table. "I probably don't need the calories, but it's Valentine's Day and life is too short to pass up brownies this good."

"Get me one too, if you don't mind." Drake turned and watched as she put the generous squares of brownies on their paper towels and handed one to him. "Gracie has a gluten allergy, so I have to get special brownie mixes and special spaghetti and things like that. I can honestly say that around here we like the gluten-free brownies the best. They stick to your ribs."

"Oh yeah. I forgot she had that." Esther turned and walked into the living room with Drake. "Is it hard cooking special foods for her?"

"No." Drake sat down on the old love seat and stretched his shoulders. "We all just eat the gluten-free stuff too. It's not hard, but specialty foods cost more. Everything tonight was gluten-free, even the rolls."

"You know what, Drake?" Esther sat down across from him, taking care not to spill her coffee as she straightened the hem of her dress.

"What's that?" He leaned back and set the paper towel on his knee.

"You are pretty amazing."

"I thought you were going to tell me something important about gluten the way you sounded," Drake said, smiling as he sipped his coffee. "I'm not amazing. I'm just doing what has to be done to make all this work." He pinched a corner off of the brownie and put it in his mouth. "You do what you have to do."

"I guess." Esther took a sip of coffee. "I deal with a lot of kids and a ton of parents, and believe me, not everyone puts their children first the way you do. It's sad really."

"I can't imagine it any other way." Drake stretched his legs out in front of him, holding on to the paper towel so it wouldn't slip off his lap. "When Paige died, I was a mess. God got me through it, but there were days when I wanted to throw my hands up and give in. Molly wasn't even a year old, and Gracie was always sick to her stomach back then before we figured out what her problem was. Momma helped, but her way of doing things is not always my way." He sipped his coffee again. "I don't want to sound ungrateful, because I'm really not. She always came through in the crunches, but Momma's not a believer."

"Yeah." Esther picked up her brownie. "I remember that none of your family ever attended church when we were kids." She took a bite and licked a crumb from her lips. "I guess that makes it hard trying to raise your children to love God when your mother influences them so much."

"It does. She doesn't intentionally do anything to sabotage what I teach them. She just tells them things like, most people can do fine without as much God as your daddy seems to think you need. She plans things for them on Sundays when she knows I want them in church." Drake rolled his head around on his shoulders and pushed down a yawn. "I've tried to talk to her about it, but she really thinks she's okay, and I'm the weird one."

"That's tough." Esther sat forward on the love seat. "You look like you're about ready to drop. I'm going to set my cup in the sink and get going." She wrapped the uneaten half of the brownie in the paper towel. "I'm taking this with me, though. I may switch to gluten-free brownies too. These are so good."

"You don't have to rush off." Drake sat up, putting his cup and paper towel on the coffee table. "This coffee will kick in after a couple of minutes, and I'll have my second wind."

"No." Esther stood. "I don't want to wear out my welcome."

"Look." Drake stood and pushed his lips together. "I wasn't very gung-ho sounding in the grocery store when Scout invited you."

"It's okay, Drake." Esther said. "I know he sprung this on you."

"No, listen." Drake rubbed his hands across his eyes. He usually got in bed shortly after the kids, but he didn't want Esther to think he was an old grump. "I'm really glad you came tonight. I've been in my own little rut with the kids and work and dealing with everything life has thrown at me. This has been..." He looked at Esther staring at him, waiting for his next words. "I had a great time."

"Me too," Esther said, her eyes peering into Drakes.

A hint of something fluttered in Drake's chest. Something that had been missing for a long, long time. "Esther, I..."

"You don't have to handle all of this alone. I am your friend, Drake. Friends help each other. Don't forget that."

Esther leaned back in the steaming hot water and willed her shoulders to relax. A friend, that's what she had said to Drake. She was his friend. It was true, but was it fair to him, or to her, to pretend that she didn't have feelings for him beyond that?

"What was I supposed to say?" Esther leaned her head against the cool, hard surface of her claw-footed tub, her hair fanning out around her. "Drake, I know you only invited me over because I trapped you into it, but I've had a crush on you since middle school, so wrap them muscled arms around me and kiss me like I've always dreamed about." She puffed out her cheeks and sank deeper into the water, pulling her head completely under. A couple of seconds later, she pushed back up, her soppy curls wilting against her face. "Who am I kidding? He's so wrapped up in his kids... as he should be." She laid her head against the back of the tub and stared at the twelve-foot-high ceiling. "He'll never have time for a woman in his life, and if he does, why would it be me?"

Thirty minutes later, Esther climbed out of the now tepid water and slipped into her flannel pajamas. She padded down the stairs to the kitchen and looked at the counter where she had left the rest of her brownie wrapped in the paper towel. "Barlow." Esther yelled through the old house. "Where's my brownie?" She flipped her head forward and re-wrapped the towel around her wet curls, then stood back up. Her brother leaned against the door frame leading into the dining room. "I hope you haven't eaten my brownie," she said, her hands on her hips.

"You left it out like you didn't want it." Barlow grinned at his sister with brown eyes identical to her own. "Besides, you'd already eaten half of it. It wasn't that good, anyway."

"Are you kidding me?" Esther raised her eyebrows and stepped over to the silver refrigerator and jerked open the door. "You know it was good, and you ought to be ashamed of yourself for eating my food."

"But you know I'm not." Barlow pushed off the door and stepped up behind his sister, looking over her shoulder into the fridge. "Where have you been, anyway? Honor and Callie had pizza at their house this evening for our Sunday school class. It was a last-minute thing. I left a message for you to stop by, but I never heard back."

"I had plans." Esther slammed the refrigerator door and

opened the cabinet beside it. "I haven't checked my messages, but I couldn't have gone."

"Where'd you go?" Barlow reached over Esther's shoulder and pulled out the package of Oreos. "Pour us some milk."

Esther grabbed two glasses, poured the milk, and walked to the living room where her brother was lounging in the recliner. Barlow had also gone to nursing school and was a nurse practitioner like her, but his career path had been very different from her own. She worked Monday through Friday at the Children's Clinic, but Barlow practically lived in the emergency room, thriving on the critical care situations that came through the hospital doors. They had bought this house together from their grandparents several years ago when they finished college and decided to stay in Carson's Bayou to work. They promised each other that when one of them got married, they would not kick the other to the curb, but would let the single sibling stay until they found another place to live, then buy their part of the house from them. Now, here they were, almost thirty, sitting at home on Valentine's night eating Oreos and drinking milk.

"So." Barlow took the glass of milk from Esther and dunked his cookie. "Where were you tonight?"

"I was over at Drake's house."

"Drake?" Barlow shoved the entire cookie into his mouth and reached for another one. "What were you doing there? One of his kids hurt or something?"

"No." Esther nibbled the corner of her cookie, not really wanting it. "He asked me over for dinner, and I said yes."

"Alright, Sis. We had this talk fifteen years ago. I guess it's time to have it again. Drake Lewis is not for you."

"First of all," Esther stared at her brother. "I'm not a kid anymore, and who I date is none of your business. Second of all." She shoved the cookie into her milk. "He's not who he was back then. He's a really nice guy."

"Drake's always been a nice guy. That's not the problem."

"Let it go, Barlow." Esther pulled the soggy cookie from the milk, and it broke off, disappearing to the bottom of her glass. "Besides, it wasn't a date or anything like that. His son, Scout, asked me to come over. I went because Drake's an old friend." Her eyebrows pulled low, and she frowned down into her milk glass. "But I wanted that brownie I brought home with me." She set her glass down on the end table beside her.

"Well, before you start getting too friendly with Drake, you'd better think about all the baggage he has attached to him." Barlow popped another cookie into his mouth. "I'm not trying to be mean. You know Drake and I are friends. The guy has just got a lot on him, and he's kind of spinning his wheels."

"What do you mean?"

"He's raising a family on his own. I know that has to be hard, but he had a good career working construction and gave it all up. He manages the hardware store, Esther. What kind of future is there in that?"

"He doesn't want to be away from his kids," Esther said, crossing her arms across her chest. "That's a good thing, Bar. You can't raise your kids if you're always away somewhere working."

"All I'm saying is, you'd better think long and hard before jumping off into that."

"It was one dinner." Esther stood and snatched up her milk glass. "Geesh." She stomped back to the kitchen and poured the milk in the sink, the mushy Oreo oozing down the drain. *It doesn't matter. Even if I did want to go out with him, he's not interested in me.*

Chapter Six

"Let me look at that, son." Drake tilted Scout's head toward the lamp and examined his child's swollen left eye, deep red and purple. "I can't believe you got into a fight."

Scout leaned back against the couch and crossed his arms over his chest, silent.

"When the school called earlier and said one of you was suspended, I never dreamed it was you. Seeing you outside of the principal's office next to that kid with his puffed-up lip really caught me by surprise."

Scout continued to stare straight ahead; his jaw clamped like a vise. Drake stepped into the kitchen and pulled a pack of green peas from the freezer. He wrapped them in a worn kitchen towel forever stained orange with tomato sauce and returned to where Scout continued to wait. "Here." He gently laid the cold compress against his son's eye. "Now, do you want to tell me what happened? Did somebody make fun of you for playing the piano?"

"No." Scout held the peas in place with his hands, not looking at his father with his one good eye. "Landon said

Gracie smells like a dog, and Molly needs a decent haircut." Scout pulled in a haggard breath. "He said we looked like trash because we don't have a momma."

"Son." Drake sat down on the couch beside his son and wrapped his arm around the boy's shoulders. "You listen to me. There will always be people coming along saying things that aren't true. They say unkind things about other people, usually because they have something hurtful in their own lives. You have to learn to ignore that kind of talk. Don't let it get to you."

"Dad." Scout hiccuped as a tear ran down his cheek. He leaned into Drake's side. "Why did God take our momma? Did we do something wrong?"

"No, son." Drake pulled back and looked his son in the face. "You listen to me. Sometimes God does things I don't understand, but there is one thing that is always true. God works things out for the good. Sometimes seeing the good is hard, but we have to keep looking, or the devil will drag us down."

"I think the devil was using Landon to drag me down today." Scout ran the back of his hand across his drippy nose. "I got so mad that I hit him, then I hit him again. I thought I would feel happy when I made him take it back, but I didn't."

"No." Drake reached over and raked a strand of sandy brown hair away from his son's forehead. "His words were hurting you, and they are still there, even when he took them back. You have to first ask yourself if what Landon said was true. If it's not, then you can't let a lie bother you."

"Dad."

"Yeah."

"Can we take Molly to a real hair cutting place? Mawmaw can cut mine and Gracie's hair, but Landon is right about Molly's hair. She needs a real haircut."

"Sure, son." Drake leaned back on the couch. "We can swing that."

Quinn opened the front door and stared at Scout, leaning against his father with his black eye and tear stained face. "What in the world happened to you, little man?" Rambler ran in around Quinn and nudged his head into Scout's lap. Quinn looked over at Drake. "I saw your truck was home and figured I'd come over and see if you wanted to help me change my oil," he said, stepping over to the couch. "But I see you've got your hands full."

"He had a little run in at school," Drake said, sitting up straighter on the couch.

"Let Uncle have a look." Quinn reached down and slipped his fingers under Scout's chin, lifting his head to examine his shiner. Scout pulled the peas away and grinned, all remorse suddenly gone from his demeanor. "Boy, somebody pegged you good. I hope you knocked them into the next county."

"It was Landon Fischer," Scout said, wincing as Quinn ran his finger over the child's swollen lid. "I popped his lip, and now he has a loose tooth."

"Good for you." Quinn grazed his knuckles across Scout's chin. "Maybe me and your dad can show you a few boxing moves in case ole Landon wants a round two. Did you get three days?"

"Quinn." Drake glared at his little brother, then looked down at his son. "Scout, go to your room and lie down. I'll call you when you can come out. Getting suspended is not a good thing."

"Yes, sir." Scout's shoulders drooped as he stood. "Bye Uncle Quinn."

"I'll smuggle you a snack before I leave," Quinn said, winking at Scout. "I'm not scared of the warden."

Scout's bedroom door closed, and Drake leaned back on

the couch. "Don't encourage him, Quinn. He's got to learn to handle junk without getting into fistfights."

"Aww, Big Brother. A little scuffle on the playground is no big deal. Look at us. We fought every boy in our class, and I think you even fought a couple of girls. We didn't end up in the pen."

"My goals are a little higher for Scout than staying out of prison."

Quinn flopped down on the love seat and patted his stomach. Rambler jumped into his lap. "You know what I mean. What's the matter with you lately? You are turning into a grouchy old man."

"Get that dog off my furniture." Drake sat forward and rolled his eyes. "No wonder I can't get Gracie to mind me about letting the dog in the house. You've got to start being a better example for the kids, Quinn. No more undermining what I tell them."

"Well." Quinn stood, and the dog slid back onto the floor. "I can see it's about time for me to head back across the road. Come on, Rambler. Somebody around here needs an attitude adjustment."

"Nothing is wrong with my attitude." Drake watched his little brother walk over and open the front door. A cool breeze blew in, and a piece of junk mail laying on the coffee table flew to the floor. "I'm trying to teach my children. I can't do that when you and Momma are always going against what I say."

"I'll talk to you later, Drake." Quinn stepped through the door behind his dog. "You don't want to hear what I'm wanting to say, and I don't want you to beat the snot out of me for saying it."

Drake watched the door close, then leaned his head back against the couch. *Lord, show me the good. I'm having a hard time seeing it right now.*

"JUST TEXT HIM AND ASK HIM." Darcy Carson pushed a red curl back from her forehead and stared across the little table in the Bayou Bean. "What have you got to lose?"

"What if he thinks I'm fishing for another date?" Esther took a sip of her caramel latte. "I guess I am, but I don't want him to *think* I am."

"What if he thinks you really liked the brownies and want to know where you can get the mix?" Darcy raised an eyebrow. "Come on, Esther. You've had a crush on this guy since junior high and had a great time last week. Be the fearless Esther that I know and love."

"Hmph." Esther pushed her lips together. "That's easy for you to say. I remember a few years back when you were whining about going out with Blaze. He was practically throwing himself at you before you would give him the time of day."

"See what I mean?" Darcy smiled. "You're making my point. We turned out great, all because I finally took a chance."

"Okay." Esther pulled in a puff of air and blew it out. "What's the worst that could happen? He could tell me to leave him alone and quit bringing the kids to the clinic and have me picked up for stalking."

"Oh, girl, please." Darcy said. "You are being ridiculous. Send the text already."

Esther took her phone from her purse and pulled up the number Scout had given her that evening in the grocery store.

> Drake, this is Esther Sartin. I was wondering if you could tell me where you get the gluten-free brownie mix. I really liked them and want to make some more.

Esther bit her lower lip as her finger hovered over the button. "Here goes nothing." She hit send and lay the phone down and picked back up her coffee. "He probably won't..."

Bzzzz. Esther's eyes stretched wide. She looked at the phone, then up at Darcy, then back at the phone.

"We are worse than a couple of junior high kids," Darcy laughed. "Pick up your phone, goofy."

> Hey, Esther. I was just thinking about you. I need some help with a little problem. If we could meet this afternoon when we get off work, I will give you a brownie mix in exchange for a bit of your time.

Esther touched her hand to her mouth and slid her phone across the table for Darcy to read. "He was just thinking about me." Her brow wrinkled as she watched Darcy read the text. "What kind of problem is he talking about? Probably with his kids."

"He said a little problem." Darcy slid the phone back across the table. "Well?"

"Well, what?" Esther continued to frown, staring at her best friend.

"Well, don't leave him hanging. Answer the text."

"Oh. Yeah." Esther picked up the phone. *Sure.*

> That will be fine. Do you want me to come to your house?

She read the words to Darcy. "Too desperate?"

"Hit send."

Esther hit the button and pulled her lips in, biting down as she waited for his response.

> No, can we meet for coffee? Have you been to that coffee shop on the old side of town? I've never been, but I hear they make a decent cup. It's the Bayou Bean or Bayou Coffee or something like that.

Esther's lips pushed up into a smile.

> Sure. I get off at five.

Her phone buzzed again.

> See you then.

"Now what?" Esther picked up her coffee and took a sip. "Is this a date?"

"Now we finish our break and go back to the office." Darcy picked up her coffee, drained the last few drops, and set it back on the table. "At five, you drive back over here like it's no big deal... because it's not."

"But is it a date?" Esther picked up her cup then set it back down, no longer wanting the sweet drink. "Or is it just Drake meeting me for coffee to talk?"

"Why don't you quit trying to slap a label on it?" Darcy stood up from her chair and picked up her purse from where it hung on the back of the chair. "I promise, Esther. I've never seen you like this. What gives?"

"I guess I'd kind of written all of this off, you know. Esther, the single girl who lives with her twin brother, that's me." She dropped her phone into her purse and stood up. "I've always had these crazy notions of Drake in my head, but those were my dreams. I knew they would always be dreams. Now though…"

Darcy stepped around the table and squeezed her friend's shoulders. "Well, he has a problem and wants you to help him fix it. That's a start, right?"

"Yeah." Esther followed Darcy out of the Bayou Bean and got in her friend's double cab truck. *Don't make a big deal out of this. Molly might have a runny nose, and Drake didn't want to bring her in to the clinic. Of course, he would think of me first.* She sat silently as Darcy talked about Frank and Hope, her two kids. *I did tell him I was his friend and he could call on me to help him.*

They pulled into the Children's Clinic, and Esther unbuckled her seat belt. Being Drake's friend would do if that was what this was about. She shoved her expectations back down in that deep well where they belonged as they walked into the medical complex. But still…

Chapter Seven

Esther tugged down on the tank top underneath her tan scrub shirt. She sat down in the chair at the Bayou Bean for the second time that day. Her face creased with a smile as Drake slid the box of gluten-free brownie mix across the little table to her. "Aww. Thank you. That brother of mine ate the rest of my brownie the other night, and I've been wanting one ever since."

"This is the best brand." Drake tapped the top of the box. "They sell another kind at the grocery store, but they are dry and get hard as a brick. I usually buy four boxes at a time of this one so we can have brownies once a week."

Esther turned the box around and scanned the directions. Nothing special, eggs, oil, and water. "Have you ordered your coffee yet?"

"No," Drake said. "I was waiting for you. Tell me what you want, and I'll go place our orders."

Esther gave Drake her coffee order, then watched as he walked up to the counter a few feet away. He was every bit as good looking now as he had been in high school. Actually, he looked better. His shoulders filled out the gray canvas work shirt with the hardware store's logo on the pocket. He still had the same flat stomach from his earlier years. His face was a little fuller, and he had a few creases at his eyes when he smiled, but he was definitely aging well. She looked down at her top, stretched a little tighter across her chest than it had been last year. Worrying about her size was not something she did as long as her blood work was okay on her yearly checkup. She gave the top another tug. *Friends. My size doesn't matter now either. I am who I am.*

"Here ya go." Drake walked back up to the table with two saucers. "This one is filled with Bavarian cream and this one with lemon." He set the saucers of donuts in the center of the table. "They will bring the coffee in a second."

"Oh man. I was just thinking that I may have put on a winter coat like a bear and here you are bringing sweets."

"Please don't tell me that you're one of those women always watching every little morsel of food you put in your mouth, always trying to look like a ten-year-old."

"And what if I am?" Esther raised her eyebrow, a twinkle in her eyes.

"If you are, I guess I need to drag my foot out of my mouth and apologize." He pulled his chair out and sat down. "I have to tell you, though, that I don't think it's healthy for a grown woman to try to always look like a child. The older my girls get, the more concerned I get with this kind of thing." He paused as a teenage boy stepped up with their coffees and set their cups in front of them. "Let me tell you, having daughters has put some entirely new thoughts into my head that I never would have dreamed possible ten years ago."

"Before you break into a lecture on positive body images, don't worry. I've never been overly concerned with my weight. I come from a long line of curvy women. We are who we are." She reached out and slid the Bavarian cream donut to her side of the table. "That being said, diabetes runs in our family as well, so I don't go crazy with the sweets too often. I try to do active things I enjoy, like play softball with the church in the summer to get a little exercise."

"That I can understand," Drake said, a frown shadowing his face. He pulled the lemon filled donut over. "Diabetes is a legitimate concern."

"Speaking of concern." Esther picked up the sticky pastry with her fingers. "You said you have a problem?"

"Yeah. It's Scout." Drake picked up his donut, then set it back down. "Well, actually, it's all three of my kids. Scout got in a fight at school yesterday over his sisters, especially Molly and her hair."

"Oh. I'm sorry to hear that. Kids can be so cruel."

"They can be, but I don't want Scout to feel that punching a kid in the face is an acceptable response when someone is being a jerk." He picked the donut up again. "I talked to him about it and thought we had it all worked out. Then Quinn came over and started asking him how the other kid looked, then offered to teach him a few boxing moves. Today I heard Momma telling him he did the right thing. Her mantra ever since I can remember has been, don't start it, but don't take it, and always go down swinging."

Esther took a bite of her donut, and her eyes stretched wide. The cream squished out of the sides of the flaky pastry and dribbled down her chin. "Words I believe you used to live by," she said, grabbing a napkin from the silver holder on the table.

"Until I met Paige, and then came to know the Lord. I learned growing up that fighting, and bowing your chest, and being cocky, were all signs of strength. Now my momma is teaching this same philosophy to my children."

"I see why you are concerned." Esther set down her donut and wiped the sugar from her fingers. "Have you talked to her about this?"

"I have, but it's like talking to a fence post. I don't see Momma, or Quinn for that matter, changing their ways anytime soon."

"What are you going to do?"

"I honestly don't know. I don't want to drive a wedge between the kids and my mother, but they need exposure to more than just my family. The little bit they get on Sundays and Wednesdays at church is good, but it's not enough."

"How can I help?" Esther picked up her coffee and took a sip. "There are a couple of after school childcare programs here in town. Is that what you are considering?"

"No." Drake chewed on his lemon donut, then blotted his lips with his paper napkin. "That's not what I wanted help with. I might eventually have to put them in daycare, though. That's a good idea." He set down his napkin and looked at Esther. "This is going to sound silly, but it's the truth. None of my kids have ever had a real haircut. Momma sits them on the back porch every once in a while and gives them a trim. That's the way she did mine and my brothers too, still does." He glanced down at his napkin, then back up at Esther. "She does fine on all of our straight hair, but Molly's hair, well, I think she might need it done by a professional. You know." He nodded his head toward Esther. "Yours is really curly, but I don't ever remember it looking as crazy as Molly's does."

"You want me to take Molly to get her hair done?" Esther's brow furrowed. She wasn't sure what she was expecting, but this wasn't it. "I guess I can do that."

"I would come with you, you know, to make sure Molly didn't throw a fit or kick anybody." Drake picked up his coffee cup. "Actually, I might get Gracie's done too. I bet she would like that. What do you think?"

"Do you really want the girls to have a good time?" Esther's eyes sparkled as a plan formed in her head. "I have an idea."

"Sure." A dimple appeared in Drake's chin as he smiled. "You look like the cat that swallowed the canary. What are you grinning about?"

"It's a way to help with your other problem too, if you're game."

"Let's hear it."

"Why don't you and I plan on taking the kids out to do some things a couple of times a month? Simple things like haircuts and shoe shopping, or whatever is on your agenda for that month. Maybe I can even take them to get their toenails done before summer... my treat. That way, they can have a woman's influence in their lives to compare with your mother's, and you get a little help dealing with your children, too." She looked down at the last bite of the donut on her plate, then cut her eyes up to Drake. "I saw how tired you all were at the grocery store that evening. You could all use a little outside help every now and then."

"That's sounds great on my end, but what's in it for you?" Drake wadded up his napkin and threw it on his plate. "I love my kids, but let's face it, the girls can be a handful and even Scout can when he gets an idea in his head."

"It's a couple of times a month." Esther reached her finger up and rubbed it across the corner of her mouth where a flake of powder sugar was waiting. "We're friends. I like kids, and I told you I would help you. Let me do this."

"I don't know, Esther. This seems a little one-sided."

"Okay, then. What can you offer to me to even the deal?" Esther smiled. "I enjoy free brownies and spaghetti."

"Let me think on it," Drake said, watching Esther. "If you're serious. I say let's try it a couple of times. Heaven knows the kids will benefit from being around you."

"Alright then," Esther said. "I will get in touch with my hairdresser and see if we can bring in the girls this weekend."

"Alright. It's a date."

Drake opened his eyes and looked at the moonlight coming through the living room window. When he got back from talking with Esther and picking the kids up at his mother's, he only had an hour before it was time to put them in bed. They had already eaten, so he spent the time going over homework and making sure everyone took their baths and brushed their teeth. Sometime after the last goodnight, when he sat down on the couch to catch a breath, he had dozed off.

What time is it? He stretched his eyes wide and lay his head back on the couch. The idea of having Esther along for the girls' haircuts seemed promising. *What do you tell a beautician when you bring your daughter to them with her hair all jacked up? Fix it? Yeah, I'm definitely out of my element.*

His mother had not been too happy about the plans when he told her that evening. "You're throwing perfectly good money away at a beauty shop, son. If you want to toss your money to the wind, give it to me instead."

Momma's wrong. Maybe, after they were done with the kids' hair, they could get a donut like he had done with Esther tonight. She had looked so cute with the cream filling on her cheek. The kids needed to learn how to sit still in a place like the coffee shop, anyway. It would be good for them to go out in public and sit at a table... with him and Esther.

Drake reached up and rubbed the whiskers on his jawline. *What can I give back to Esther for all the time she's giving up helping the kids? Free handyman services?* Sarah Franklin did that for Scout's piano lessons. *Nah. That's not right.* No. He would have to think about it. It needed to be something special for

Esther. She was giving of herself. She was so good with the kids, even Molly.

He stood and stretched his back, then made his way toward his bedroom. Esther sitting across the table from him at the Bayou Bean, her caramel curls escaping from the clip at her neck. Esther, laughing at something he said, all played through his mind as he sat down to pull off his work shoes. *She's a beautiful woman with a great sense of humor and smart as a whip. Why isn't she married?* He'd never really given it any thought. Of course, he hadn't given much thought about anything since Paige died. *I'll talk to Esther, but I won't interfere in her personal life. If I have to, I will find another way to handle this problem with the kids.*

He pulled one boot off, then the other. *She said she was alone on Valentine's night, so she might be between boyfriends. Being picky is a good thing. She deserves a nice guy.* If she would do this with him until she started dating someone, that would be all he could expect from her. *Yeah, I need to talk to her about that.* The way she looked when she stood up from the table, her figure filling out her nursing scrubs perfectly.... *No, she won't be hanging out with us for long.*

Chapter Eight

"Mawmaw says you are being ridiculous, Daddy."

"Mawmaw does not know everything, little girl." Drake buckled Molly into her booster seat. "We are going to give this a try, aren't we, Gracie?" He looked at his middle child, already buckled in between her two siblings. "And we are going to be nice to Miss Esther, as well. She set this up for you two out of the goodness of her heart."

"Yes, Daddy." Gracie nodded, her face wreathed in smiles. "I want bangs like my friend Casey. Do you think I can get bangs? Mawmaw won't cut bangs for me."

"I'm sure you can have bangs, big girl." Drake patted Gracie's knee clad in pink leggings, her sparkly Mary Janes bobbing up and down. Poor child. He should have been more attentive to how important this was to her. She was practically glowing with anticipation. "See, Molly." He looked at the frowning four-year-old. "It's going to be fun."

"I'm not gonna like it." Molly crossed her arms over her chest and kicked the back of the front seat.

"Girl, you look just like your momma, but I promise, you

act just like Uncle Quinn sometimes." Drake reached down and put his hand on her ankle, stopping her red cowboy boot from kicking the seat. "Are you going to be good? Or are you going to get yourself in trouble, end up in your bed for the entire evening, and still get the haircut anyway?"

"Be good." The words squeezed out through Molly's clenched jaw. She huffed and crossed her arms over her chest. "I hate beauty shops."

Drake climbed into the front seat of his old truck and headed into town. He pulled into the light gray two-story house with the black shutters and a manicured front lawn. It was a far cry from his house with half of the screen torn off the front door where Gracie sneaked in Rambler and Poochie every chance she got. Their sparse grass, mudholes, and broken toys scattered about their front yard looked almost like a war zone. Esther, dressed in blue jeans, a pink pullover sweater and sneakers, stepped off the wrap around front porch and hurried to the truck.

Drake slipped out of the driver's side and met her, opening the passenger's side door for her. "You and Barlow have your grandparent's place looking nice. I sometimes get out this way doing handy work. Every time I drive by, I always remember that time Barlow and I climbed out that second-story window and your pawpaw came out in his drawers with a gun, thinking somebody was snooping on his property."

"It's a wonder Papaw didn't get you two with rat shot." Esther slid into the truck seat and looked over her shoulder. "Hey you three. Gracie, you are so pretty in your unicorn shirt. I love the sequins."

"It's my favorite." Gracie smiled at Esther. "I'm wearing my sparkly shoes, too. Do you think the hair cut lady will like them?"

"She will love them." She smiled at Scout, who returned

her smile, then she twisted around to talk to the little rain cloud behind her. "Hello, Molly."

"I don't like beauty shops." Molly's brow scrunched in a frown.

"Remember our talk," Drake said, sliding behind the steering wheel and looking at his youngest daughter's stormy face in the rear-view mirror. "We are going to have a good afternoon. Since it's not rainy and nasty, if everyone behaves, we can go get a donut at the coffee place afterwards if Miss Esther has time. I checked, and they have a donut Gracie can eat."

"I have all the time in the world." Esther pulled her seat-belt across her chest and buckled in. "I noticed that the little snow cone place is already open too. If the kids would rather, we can get a snow cone and go to the park instead."

"Park, Dad... please." Scout leaned forward as Drake pulled onto the street and started across town to the salon. "We never get snow cones."

"Park it is." A few minutes later, Drake pulled the truck into an open spot in front of Sissy's Sassy Cuts. Esther had discussed the salon with Gracie during the ride, gradually pulling Molly into the conversation and lightening her mood. She really was good with the kids.

"Look at you." A tall, pencil thin woman with silver blond hair and a streak of blue through the side stepped from behind an empty black salon chair and walked toward the group entering the glass front door of the business. Although the waiting area wasn't very spacious, the back area where the cutting took place was long and narrow, with six chairs, three on either side. Mirrors seemed to be everywhere, and the place appeared much larger than it was. "Are these the beautiful Lewis girls I've been hearing about?" The woman, probably in her forties, smiled down at the kids, her black apron tied around her tiny waist, suntanned legs sticking out of blue jean capris below with rhinestone encrusted flip flops on her feet. "And you must be the handsome big brother. What happened to that eye?"

"I'm Scout. It's a whole lot better now."

"That's quite a shiner." The beautician reached down and pulled her fingers through a few strands of Scout's hair. "We can tighten your hair up a little too while you're here. Mandy and Lisa are both open right now, so it won't take any longer." She glanced up at Drake. "If it's okay with Dad."

"Can I, Dad?" Scout looked up at Drake. "I want it to be like that." He pointed to a picture on the wall of a boy with clipped hair on the sides and a little longer on top. "Please."

"Why not?" *Do they really feel different from the other kids at school?* Drake looked down at his son's simple bowl cut. His son was probably the only child in his class with the outdated haircut. *I've got to do better.*

Gracie and Scout climbed into two other hairdresser's chairs and Sissy, the blue-haired lady, looked down at Molly, her arms wrapped securely around her father's leg, thumb planted in her mouth. "Now, precious, I think we are going to have to wash your curls before we cut them." She reached out her hand. "You ready?"

"No." Molly grabbed Drake's leg even tighter. "I'm not doing it. I don't want a snow cone."

"Oh, baby." The hairdresser squatted in front of Molly. "I cut Miss Esther's hair all the time and her hair is just as curly as yours. I promise it's not bad. It's even kind of fun."

"No." Molly kicked her cowboy boot in Sissy's direction and the woman stood up, eyes wide. "We might have to wait until another day."

"Molly." Esther squatted down beside the child, her hand gently caressing her wild hair. "If I get my hair washed and trimmed in the chair beside yours, will you get yours done too? We can be twins, like me and my brother."

"Except I have the prettiest hair." Molly pulled her thumb out of her mouth, mulling over the suggestion. "Will my hair hang down like yours instead of sticking up?"

"It will if you let Miss Sissy wash it and put her magic tonic in it," Esther said. "I put magic tonic in mine every morning."

"Really?" Molly's eyes stretched wide, and she released her death grip on Drake's leg.

"Really."

Drake watched, slowly shaking his head as Esther took Molly's hand, and they walked to the back of the shop. *She's amazing. I have to think of something special to repay her for this. What though? Her house and job are both better than anything I'll ever have. What in the world can I offer her she can't get for herself?*

A few minutes later Drake watched Molly, her hair freshly washed, climb onto the booster seat in the salon chair, her face creased in smiles.

"You look like a sad clown," Molly said, watching Esther sit in the seat beside her. Black streaks of mascara streamed down Esther's cheeks where the water had gotten on her face. Both Molly's and Esther's curls stuck up in all directions, having just been toweled dry.

"And you look like a happy clown," Esther said, wiggling her nose at Molly. Esther's eyes met Drake's in the mirror's reflection.

"Thank you." Drake mouthed the words to Esther. She smiled in return, and a warmth filled Drake's chest, a warmth that had not been there in a very, very long time.

The heat rushed up Esther's neck as she looked in the

mirror. Sad clown, Molly pegged that one. Black mascara ran down her face in puddles. Waterproof. Why hadn't she put on waterproof mascara? *So much for impressing him with my looks.* She smiled at Molly's reflection in the mirror and pushed down the knot in her throat. Drake stared at her reflection in all its runny make-up, red-faced, frizzy-haired glory. She forced her lips into a smile, and her heart melted as she read the words on his silent lips. The forced smile fell away along with the dread of her reflection, and a warm glow took its place. This day was not about her... well, maybe it had started out that way. She looked to her right at Molly, preening as the beautician sprayed her hair and started smoothing out her curls. Her gaze pulled to the reflection directly behind her where one beautician was clipping the sides of Scout's hair, and the other was trimming Gracie's bangs as she chattered away about Quinn's dog.

No, if she was going to do this, she needed to get her head straight. These kids needed normal experiences that apparently were lacking since their mother had died. She turned her head and looked at Drake's reflection. The love on his face as his eyes took in the joy his children were getting from the outing tugged at her heart. Would this be enough for her? *What if he always sees me as a friend, a person to help with his kids?*

"You don't need a haircut this soon, Esther."

Esther smiled as Sissy leaned down and whispered in her ear. She glanced over at Molly, who was smiling at them both. "Can you pretend?"

"I'll get Jazmine to come and do that," Sissy said, smiling at Molly's peering eyes as she continued to speak. "She's in the back sweeping up. Do you mind if she combs you out? She's almost out of beauty school, and I'll be right here beside you."

"That's perfect." Esther looked over at Molly as Sissy

stepped to the back to get her daughter. "What do you think so far?"

"My hair smells like Jolly Ranchers," Molly said, stretching one of her yellow blond curls to her nose. "This is the best day ever."

Yeah, she could do this. Drake had his hands full, his life full. If this was the only way she could fit into his world, then so be it. Some things were more important than what her heart wanted. "You know what, Molly? I think you're right."

"Miss Esther." Molly leaned toward Esther and waved her arm for Esther to lean in. Esther leaned as close as she dared without tipping out of the chair. "Will you buy me some of the magic spray so my hair will look like yours? It's important to me."

"Yes, Molly." Esther smiled. "I can tell it's important to you. I'll get Miss Sissy to teach you how to use it, too. It only takes a little. Do you have a comb with the wide teeth like she's using?"

"Teeth?" the child's forehead wrinkled. "We have a brush and daddy keeps a comb in his pocket."

Poor baby. No wonder she was always a frizzy mess. "I'll get you a special comb for our kind of hair, too. If you or your daddy have any trouble with your curls, you have him call me. I'll be happy to help you."

"Miss Esther?"

"Yes, Molly?"

"I love you."

Chapter Nine

Esther, smiling, sat on the park bench. Drake stood across the way, pushing Molly on the nearby swing. Scout and Gracie climbed on the seesaw, each with their snow cones in hand. Esther peered up at the bright blue afternoon sky and pulled in a deep, satisfying breath of air. You had to love Louisiana winters. It was sixty-five degrees, and beautiful sunshine at the end of February. This month was always a wildcard. You might get ice and snow for half a second, or you might get sun and flip-flops, or like this year, a mash up of both.

"You are right." Drake stepped up to the bench and smiled down at Esther's upturned face. "This is much better than the coffee shop." He sat down beside her and poked his spoon around in his snow cone. "What are you thinking, looking so relaxed like that?"

"Two things." Esther looked at his snow cone cup and shivered. "One, I love living in Carson's Bayou, and I'm glad my parents moved back here when I was little."

"And?"

"And, who in their right mind orders a dill pickle flavored

snow cone?" Her upper lip turned up, and her nostrils flared. "You know that thing has to be nasty."

"Have you ever tried one?" Drake held a spoonful of the crushed ice under her nose, tinted a pale green with the pickle juice. "Here, just one little bite, and you will never go back to. What was it? Strawberry shortcake?"

"No, thank you." Esther pushed his hand away and laughed. "Strawberry cheesecake. There is a difference." She stuck out her tongue as he shoved the spoon in his mouth and grinned. "Agh. You're killing me."

"Come on." Drake wiggled his eyebrows and scooped up another spoonful. He leaned in closer, putting the spoon to her lips. "One little bite."

"You need to stop." Esther laughed, leaning away from Drake's spoon, his face closer to hers than it had ever been. Her heart danced as she studied his mischievous eyes.

"Daaaad." Molly's voice broke into Esther's happy bubble, and Drake sat back up, looking to where Molly sat on the swing, staring at them. "I need you over here with me."

"I'll be there in a minute." Drake held up his Styrofoam cup. "I'm taking a break to eat my snow cone." He looked back at Esther. "I can't get over how great her hair looks. Gracie's and Scout's look good too, but Molly looks like a different kid."

"She is so proud." Esther looked into her Styrofoam cup at the deep red ice, giving her emotions a chance to smooth out. "Fixing it is not hard either. Just make sure you use conditioner when you wash it, then blot it dry with the towel, spritz it, and run your fingers through it. Please don't pull a brush through it or it will frizz to high heaven, no matter how it's cut."

"We'll figure it out. I may have to FaceTime you a couple of times until we get it right."

"That will be..."

An ear-piercing scream cut through Esther's thoughts, and her eyes darted to the swings. Molly sat on the ground on Scout's end of the seesaw. Scout stood over her, glaring down at his sister with blue snow cone, Molly's bubblegum snow cone, all over his head and chest. Gracie, sobbing on the other end of the seesaw, sitting half on half off, her snow cone spilled all over her shirt, glared murderously at Molly.

Esther stood, but Drake was already scooping up Gracie and heading to the other two children by the time she made it to the seesaw, his voice bellowing across the sunny play area.

"But Dad." Scout's tear-filled eyes looked up at Drake. "She dumped it on my head, and I didn't do anything."

"I don't care, son." Drake reached down with his empty arm and helped Molly stand, her eyebrows pulled low, defiance shooting from her eyes. "She's only four. You can't be rough with her."

"I wasn't, Dad." Scout's frustrated voice grew louder. "I jumped off the seesaw, and she fell. I didn't..."

"Young man, you'd better watch that tone." Drake stared down at his son as Gracie lifted her head from his shoulder, her face streaked with tears.

"He didn't do nothing, Daddy. It was Molly," Gracie said.

"Was not." Molly stomped her foot and stuck her tongue out at her sister.

"Here." Esther took Gracie's empty snow cone cup from the child's hand and handed her the almost full strawberry cheesecake cup. "Let's trade. I've had all I wanted, anyway."

"Really?" Gracie smiled at Esther, her tears forgotten, as Drake put her back on the ground. "Thank you, Miss Esther."

"What about mine?" Molly looked at Esther. "It's gone too."

"I don't think..."

"Scout, pour half of yours in Molly's cup," Drake said, cutting Esther off.

Esther's eyes narrowed. She frowned as Scout obeyed his father without voicing anymore protests. Molly eyed her brother as he poured his snow cone into her cup, her face smug.

That's just plain wrong. "Can I talk to you for a minute... in private?" Esther asked, watching Gracie and Molly go back to the swings. Scout sat on the seesaw, his chin tucked down and arms crossed over his chest.

"Y'all finish up," Drake said over his shoulder, following Esther back to the bench. "We're leaving in a second before Scout and Gracie get cold."

They stepped up to the bench, and Drake turned to Esther. "Sorry about that. They get a little wild sometimes."

"You were wrong." Esther heard the anger in her voice, but right now, she didn't really care how she sounded. Drake Lewis was acting like a blind imbecile where his youngest child was concerned.

"Excuse me?"

"That was not Scout's fault. Molly provoked him."

The muscles in Drake's jaw visibly tightened. "I appreciate your concern, Esther, but I've been doing this parenting thing for a few years now and..."

"And if this is how you're doing it, it's no wonder Molly acts the way she does."

"What exactly does that mean?" Drake's eyes narrowed as he stared down at Esther, stepping in closer.

"Don't bully me, Drake." Esther stared back, her head stretched upward, sparks shooting from her eyes. "You are wrong, and I'm not scared of you, not even a little." She poked her finger into his chest. "So back off."

"I'm not trying to scare you." Drake took a step backward, but his eyes never left hers. "You are talking about things you don't understand," he said, his voice low, tight with restraint. "I think it's time I took you home."

"Fine, but you listen to me." Angry tears filled Esther's eyes. She blinked them away. "You are alienating your son and turning that cute little girl into a monster nobody wants to be around. If you think that's okay, then you need to think again."

The ride back to her house was as quiet as a tomb. The children, even though full of sugar, didn't make a peep. Esther stared straight ahead until the truck pulled into her driveway. She unbuckled her seatbelt and turned, looking at the three sad faces. "I had a very good time today." Her eyes traveled from one child to the next, all three faces full of remorse over how the day had ended.

"I'm sorry I ruined our trip," Scout said, his lower lip quivering.

"Oh, Scout." Esther reached across the seat and cupped his cheek in her hand. "You don't have to apologize to me." She reached up and touched his freshly cut hair. "Do you think the kids at school will like your new cut?"

"Yes, ma'am." He smiled softly. "Do you like it?"

"I love it," Esther said.

"Can we go to the park again?" Molly asked, looking at Esther and Scout, all her haughtiness gone.

"I'm not sure," Esther said, her smile sad as she looked at Molly, the child's beautiful eyes searching Esther's. Esther reached over and patted Gracie's leg. "I'd better go." Gracie pushed her lips into a silent smile.

Esther slid off the seat and shut the door, looking at

Drake through the glass. He stared straight ahead, and her heart ached. What had happened to their beautiful day? Her feet dragged up the sidewalk as the forlorn family pulled away. She turned as the vehicle disappeared down the street.

This sort of scenario had never entered her mind when she decided to insert herself into the lives of Drake and the kids. *I couldn't just keep my mouth shut and watch him make a mess of disciplining his children. I might as well have agreed with the way he handled Molly's horrible behavior if I did that.*

She shouldn't have lost her cool... obviously, but how could he not see how one-sided he was being in his actions toward his daughter, how unfair it was to blame the whole thing on Scout. Poor boy. She climbed the steps to her porch and sat down in the swing on the end of the house shaded with the giant water oak, the tree Drake and Barlow had climbed out of all those years ago.

Barlow was her only sibling, and being a twin, their parents had probably handled them a little differently from other parents. Until high school, when Barlow started excluding her from his outings with the Lewis boys, she had always been neck-deep in every bit of trouble he was in. True, he usually instigated their little excursions into naughtiness, but she was always an eager participant. Her parents never cut her any slack when they caught her and Barlow acting out, and they seemed to always get caught. Whatever punishment Barlow got, she got as well.

She pushed her toe against the porch floorboards, easing the swing back and forth in the shade. A red bird landed on the railing nearby and cocked his head, staring at her. She needed to refill the feeder hanging from the tree. "Your grandma's bird welfare system," Papaw had said, when she would come visit as a kid. When her grandparents moved into the assisted living unit and sold their house to their only two grandchildren, she had continued buying the food and keeping the birds happy.

Esther leaned her head back against the swing, reaching up and rubbing her hands over her eyes, suddenly tired. *I must be coming off all that sugar from the snow cone.* She needed to rethink this *thing*. If she kept seeing Drake and the kids, the kids were going to become attached to her. They already were. What if she couldn't deal with all of this? What if Drake decided he didn't need her in his kids' lives? Pulling out would make the kids feel like she was abandoning them. That would be the worst thing for the children. She leaned forward and dropped her head in her hands. As mad as Drake had been, she didn't have to worry about any of this, anyway. He would not be letting her back around his family again, might even request she not see them at the clinic.

Drake. That ship just sailed. A sadness squeezed her heart. This was for the best. She had been dabbling in a fantasy that was never going to happen. Barlow was right. Drake had too much going on, too many differences for her to deal with at this stage of her life.

She stood up and rubbed her fingers along her lips. He had been so happy today, toying with her on the park bench. She could see them together... in a different time... in different circumstances... circumstances that could never happen now. The tears, the ones that had been wanting to fall since the argument, trickled down her face as she opened her front door.

"Hey, sis. I..." Barlow looked up from where he was sitting on the couch watching a football game. "What's wrong, Esther?" He stood and strode across the living room, wrapping his arms around her. "I tried to warn you."

Esther's shoulders shook as she let the heartache of her lifelong love pour out of her. The flicker of the dream that had ignited on Valentine's Day flickered out.

"I can go beat him up if you want me to." Barlow stepped back and lifted Esther's face from his shoulder. "Well, not really. I can go pick a fight with him and let him beat the daylights out of me, though." He smiled down at his sister, tenderness in his eyes. "I'd do that for you, you know."

"I know." Esther pulled in a shaky breath. "No, I like your nose too much where it is. It wouldn't do well shoved to your ear."

"I agree." Barlow put his hands on either side of Esther's shoulders. "Take a deep breath." He waited as Esther did as she was told. "Smell that? I made those brownies. Let's go drown your sorrows in chocolate and watch LSU kick Bama's pants off."

"Yeah. Let's do that." Esther followed Barlow to the kitchen and looked at the empty gluten-free brownie box laying on the counter. They wouldn't taste as good now, but nothing probably would be as good for a while. *I'll mope today. Tomorrow I will be me again. Twenty-nine-year-old me. Single me. Childless me. Loveless me.*

Chapter Ten

"What is wrong with you?" Quinn stared at his big brother across the engine of his truck. "You've been moody for years, but now you're plumb cranky."

Drake reached up and slammed the hood down on Quinn's shiny, smoky gray truck. "Next time, get someone else to help you change your oil."

"See. You're proving my point. Chill, brother." Quinn rolled his eyes and stepped around to the front of the truck, keeping pace with Drake as he started across the road to his house. "I ran into Barlow Sartin earlier this week, and he told me you had a run in with his sister. I told him he was blowing smoke, cause I got your back and all." Quinn leaned forward, staring at his brother's gruff face. "Is that what all this attitude is about? You sweet on Esther Sartin, and she turned you down? She thinks she's too good for you?"

"A run in?" Drake pulled up short, stopping in the middle of the gravel road running between his house and Quinn's double wide. He rubbed his hand across his jaw, staring across the road, not seeing his kids wrestling in the dirt, pouring sand on the dog. "We didn't have a run in."

It had been almost two weeks since that Saturday. Two long, miserable weeks. He had been so mad for the first four or five days that he snapped at everybody that spoke to him. Finally, last weekend, when he overheard the kids whispering about which one had to come tell him they needed toilet paper in the bathroom, the truth smacked him between the eyes. *I'm no better than Molly, pouting, acting out when I don't like things. My own kids don't want to talk to me.*

"Come on in here, you three." He had watched as they walked down the hall to his bedroom, peeking in the doorway. "Come on in. I'm done biting your heads off about everything. You can quit tip-toeing around."

Molly had been the first, coming in and jumping on the bed beside him, followed by Gracie, then Scout, easing in with a worried expression on his face. "Daddy." Scout eased onto the bed beside Drake. "Are you mad at us because we got in a fight and run off Miss Esther?"

"What?" Drake ran his hands through the top of his hair. "No, son. Y'all didn't run off Miss Esther. If anybody ran her off, it was me."

"Well, get her back, Daddy." Molly had leaned in behind Drake and wrapped her arms around his neck, clinging to his back. "She smells good and likes to talk to us."

"I like to talk to you," Drake said, leaning his face toward the child's.

"Not always, Daddy," Gracie said, sitting on the other side of Drake. "Sometimes you bark at us worse than a junkyard dog."

Drake had reached out and pulled Scout and Gracie in on top of him, tumbling back on the bed, pretending to squash Molly. "Well, this junk yard dog is ready for a tickle fight."

Things with the kids got better after that. No matter

what was going on in his head, he would not, he could not let it affect his kids. Not from now on.

"I said." Quinn stared at Drake, still standing in the middle of the road. "If that's not it, then what's going on? You don't have cancer, or something, do you? Wouldn't that beat all? Momma smokes like a train, I dip, and you get cancer."

"I don't have cancer, Quinn. And before you ask, the kids aren't sick, and I'm not going to prison or filing for bankruptcy." He started walking again. "Kids," Drake yelled toward the dust cloud in his front yard. "Quit throwing that dirt up in the air."

Quinn hurried across the road, keeping step with his brother. "I can't think of anything else, then."

"Mind your own business, Quinn," Drake said, picking Molly and Gracie up, one under each arm. "Come on Scout. Quinn, get your dog. He's not coming into the house like that."

"Are we going in the house looking like this?" Molly twisted, looking up at Drake with her eyes glowing from a face and body covered in black dirt.

"Nope." Drake headed around the house to the back porch. It was March, and the weather had been in the seventies for the past two days after a three-day cold snap at the beginning of the week. "You three are stripping down back here." He sat the girls on the porch and walked to the end of the steps. The water hose lay on the ground near a silver foot tub. He picked up the tub and shoved it onto the porch. "Strip to your drawers and come over here. I'm hosing all of you down. I don't want mud in the house, on the floor, or in our bathtub, you hear?"

Clothes and dirt went to flying in all directions, sending up another dust bowl. Gracie made it to the silver foot tub first, squealing and laughing as the cold water hit her, sending rivers of black mud into the tub. The other two kids hurried over and soon the tub was overflowing with muddy black water.

"Wait right there while I grab some towels. Do *not* go in the house." Drake dropped the hose in the foot tub and stepped over to the edge of the yard, pulling two board stiff towels from the line. He sucked in a deep breath as an icy blast of cold water hit him between the shoulders. Molly stood a few feet away, grinning like a possum in her soggy underwear, water dripping from her mop top head, the water nozzle aimed at Drake's face. "I don't think you want to do that, Molly." Drake said, putting a serious look on his face. Scout and Gracie watched from the nearby foot tub, eyes wide.

"Oh yes I do." Molly pulled the trigger, blasting Drake as he walked forward into the stream. "Stop, Daddy," she giggled. "You're supposed to stop."

"No. You're supposed to stop." Drake reached down to take the hose, and Molly dropped it, running back to the porch.

"Get Scout, Daddy, not me. I'm Momma's baby, remember?" She hopped back into the foot tub, standing behind her siblings.

"I'm not getting anybody." Drake climbed the stairs and wrapped a towel around Scout. He pulled the other one around both of the girls. "Let's go in and make some hotdogs. We need to talk about a few things."

Esther was right. Drake watched the kids run down the hall to change. He pulled a pack of little red weenies from the fridge. *She was right the minute the words came out of her mouth. That's why I got so mad. It's time to get over myself and face facts.* He pulled a beat-up old boiler from the cabinet under the microwave and stuck it under the faucet at the sink. *I'll make things right with the kids, then make things right with Esther. She probably doesn't want anything to do with me. I certainly can't blame her for that. Man, I'm a jerk, but I've got to try to fix things. If she doesn't want to see me again, maybe she will at least see the kids and let them know she's not upset with them.* He had to at least try to get her to do that, not for his sake... but for theirs.

DRAKE RUBBED his fingers against his forehead and set down on his sofa. The kids were finally asleep, and he needed to think some things through. *I need Quinn.* He probably hadn't said those words five times in his adult life, but tonight it was the truth. A lot of good it did him to say it. Quinn was offshore and would be until Sunday night. Two weeks ago, after the water hose fight in the backyard, he had talked to the kids, explaining how he wasn't fair to them, treating Molly differently, letting her get away with more than she should. They had surprised him with their insight.

"She looks like Momma's pictures, Daddy," Gracie had said. "That's why you do it."

"I don't mind taking her blame, Daddy," Scout had said, leaning against Drake's leg. "Not most of the time, anyway."

"I am the baby, Daddy." Molly had looked up at him, sympathetic to his plight like her siblings, but not quite understanding why she was the topic of their discussion.

After a long talk about fairness, forgiveness, and promises to do better, they made brownies and watched an old movie about a dog losing his boy and going across the country to find him.

Drake spent the next week texting Esther without getting a response. He dropped by the Children's Clinic to see her, but Darcy, the receptionist he had known since he was a kid, said she was too busy to take a break.

"Will you at least tell her I came by?" Drake asked,

leaning against the reception desk. "I really need to talk to her."

"If you really need to talk to her," Darcy said, stapling a stack of papers, "you'll find a way, Drake Lewis. I have never once seen somebody as hardheaded as you not doing something once they set their mind to it."

Darcy had been right, but how was he going to talk to her when she wouldn't return his phone calls or his texts, or even let him see her? Quinn would know what to do. He was sneaky and knew how to get around these kinds of problems. Quinn never would admit it, and Drake didn't care, but a lot of the fights he had gotten into as a teen were trying to protect Quinn or doling out payback to somebody bullying his little brother.

Drake flopped his head back on the sofa. Tomorrow was Saturday. He would think of some way to get her to listen to him tomorrow. His eyes drifted shut, his mind wandering to the last day he saw her. Not the stand-off, but before that. Esther taking Molly to the shampoo bowl so the child would get a haircut, turning around and talking to them in the truck, telling them how great they looked, getting snow cones.

He leaned forward and picked up his phone. He had taken a picture of Esther and the kids in front of the snow cone stand but had forgotten about it until now. He opened the photo section of his phone and looked at Esther standing between Scout and Gracie, with Molly in front of her.

> We have to get this right. I need you to know I'm sorry, I know I was a jerk. Please let me talk to you.

He finished typing the message and then added the picture.

> Please meet me at the coffee shop tomorrow at five when I get off work. I'll wait for you.

What if she didn't come? If she didn't come, well... he knew where she lived. She lived with Barlow. Drake stared at the phone, willing it to vibrate with an answer. Nothing happened. He tossed it on the couch. Well, if need be, he could get past Barlow. Barlow was a smart guy. *I can reason with him... and he knows not to tangle with me.*

Drake reached over and turned off the lamp. He needed to go get in bed, but he couldn't. He looked at the picture of Paige sitting on the end table. He loved her, always would, but honestly, for the past month, his mind had been more on Esther and how he had hurt her than on his wife. He laid down on the couch and stared at the ceiling.

Was he developing feelings for Esther? She was attractive, obviously, but now, this... whatever it was, was not about the way she looked. He closed his eyes, too tired to sort things out tonight. He would make things right with Esther... for the kids' sake, and worry about the rest later. A dog barked off in the distance and a soft woof answered from down the hall. Gracie did it again. Rambler was in the house. His mind drifted away, too tired to go put the animal out. He would deal with that later, too.

Chapter Eleven

"If you are not going to answer him, then block his number." Barlow looked down at Esther's phone vibrating on the bar. "You'd think by now he'd get the message." He pulled the stethoscope from around his neck and slid it into his scrubs pocket. "It's been a month."

"I'm..." Esther picked up her phone and slid it into her pocket. She had just walked in from her day at the clinic, and Barlow was headed out for a twelve-hour night shift at the hospital. "I'm not going to block him in case he has an emergency with his kids and needs to get in touch." She loved her brother, but really... sometimes he needed to mind his own business.

"He can go through the answering service if that happens." Barlow reached into the refrigerator and pulled out an energy drink for later. "You know that."

"I know you sure are nosy." Esther pulled the scrunchy, releasing the low ponytail at the base of her neck. "You're going to be late if you don't go."

"Alright." Barlow leaned over and draped an arm around

Esther, giving her shoulders a squeeze. "I only meddle because I saw the mess he made of you."

"I'm fine." *I will never have another meltdown in front of you as long as I live.* "I was on my period. That was most of my problem that day."

"Yeah. Sure." Barlow opened the door off of the kitchen leading to the garage. "I'll see you in the morning."

The roar of Barlow's truck driving away floated in from across the house. She pulled out her phone and stared at her latest text.

I'm at the coffee shop. Please come.

She typed in a response, then backed it out. At first, she had been too upset to talk to Drake, then too embarrassed. Now. Now she didn't know what she would say, what she would do if they met. Barlow told her he had talked to Quinn about them, and she had wanted to crawl under a stump and die. Of all the people on the planet that she wanted to be talking about her business, Quinn Lewis was at the very bottom of the list. It was best to say nothing, to stay away from Drake, and let this all blow over.

She opened the freezer and pulled out a carton of Chunky Monkey ice cream and grabbed a spoon from the drainer. She basically had the house to herself all weekend with Barlow working twelve hour nights and sleeping all day. Sometimes he even slept at the hospital. She set the ice cream on the bar to soften and went upstairs to change into her pajama pants and t-shirt. If she was going to be an old maid, might as well enjoy some of the perks. The cold water tingled against her skin as she washed her face. She smeared on the green tea mask, leaving the areas clear around her eyes and mouth, then twisted her hair up into a knot on top of her head.

Her phone buzzed again. "No, Mr. Lewis, I will not be

seeing you tonight. I have a date with Sandra Bullock and Ryan Gosling." She walked back down the stairs and picked up the ice cream. The phone buzzed again. "Good grief, Drake." She turned off her phone and left it on the bar. Barlow was right. She was not on call this weekend. If he kept texting, she was going to answer him... and see him... and want to be with him...

She grabbed the tablespoon and walked to the living room. The remote stuck her in the backside as she flopped onto the couch. She fished it out and turned on the ridiculously enormous television Barlow had put in the living room last year after Christmas. Sandra and Ryan loomed in front of her as she dug into the ice cream. She shoved a huge spoonful in her mouth as a truck motor slowed and turned into their drive. Barlow must have forgotten something. The truck stopped in the front, though. Barlow would have pulled to the back.

Knock, knock, knock. "Cheese and crackers." Esther reached up and felt the green mask dry and cracking against her skin. She hurried over to the curtain and peeked out. Drake must have knocked on the door but was now staring at the window. There was no way he didn't see the curtain move.

"Esther."

The soft crunch of footsteps floated through the window, and Esther scooted out of view behind the wall. *Just go away, Drake.*

"Esther. You don't have to let me in. Just come out and let me talk to you." He tapped on the glass, and Esther jumped, dropping the ice cream spoon on the hardwood floor. "Esther, I hear you in there. I can stand out here and do the Rocky Balboa thing if you want me to. I'm sure your neighbors would get a kick of me out here yelling."

Esther didn't move, waiting for him to yell her name... or

Adrian, whichever would be embarrassing. He would do it too, no doubt.

She didn't move, holding her breath until she couldn't in the silence. *He must have left.* She leaned around and peaked through the curtains. His truck was still there, but where was Drake? She smashed her green face against the cool window-pane and looked up and down the front porch under the shade of the giant water oak. Nope, no Drake.

A thud overhead made her stand back up straight. *He wouldn't dare.* She listened to the floor creaking above her head. *He's crazy. That crazy man is climbing in Barlow's window.* Esther grinned, an idea popping into her head. Barlow's BB gun was in the front hall closet. He kept it there in case Esther ever needed to scare off a burglar, since she refused to learn to shoot his rifle. Of course, they'd never had a burglar, but she did have an intruder. She hurried into the foyer and pulled out the little gun.

"Esther?"

She walked to the bottom of the stairs and looked up. Drake, a Taco Bell bag in one hand and a Mountain Dew in the other, descended toward her. *He brought me my favorites.* A warmth squeezed her heart, and she lowered her BB gun. "Breaking into a person's house is a good way to get shot."

"It's worth the risk." Drake stepped off the bottom step, stuck the Mountain Dew under his arm, and reached out, touching Esther's face.

Esther's pulse did a double take as his fingers brushed against her skin. She tilted her face up, looking into his eyes.

"What's this stuff?" He peeled off a strip of the mask. "It looks like dried mud out of the swamps."

Esther's hands flew up to her face—her flaky green face. "It's a mask. Sit down somewhere. I'll be right back."

"Wait." Drake grabbed her hand as she squeezed by him and started up the stairs. "We need to talk."

"Not like this we don't." She pulled her hand away and kept ascending the stairs. "You've waited a month. You can wait a few more minutes. If you can't, then let yourself out." She flew up the stairs and into the bathroom. The green face with the big peeling flake staring at her from the bathroom mirror looked like something from a cheesy zombie movie. *I can cry or I can laugh.* She turned on the water and stepped over to the door, cracking it to listen. Drake was doing something in the kitchen. Good. At least he hadn't left. She stepped back over and started scrubbing her face. Might as well laugh. Red eyes and green skin all in one evening might even scare off Drake Lewis.

DRAKE OPENED up the kitchen cabinets, looking for plates. He pulled out two matching plates and set them on the bar. He turned back and looked at the other plates, all exactly alike. Not five different kinds, each with their own novelty chip or crack, like at his house. He dumped Esther's burrito and crunchy taco on one and his four soft shelled tacos on the other. He pulled out two glasses, filled them with ice, and split the twenty-ounce Mountain Dew between them.

"How did you remember I like Taco Bell and Mountain Dew?"

Drake turned and smiled at Esther, her face scrubbed clean, and her hair hanging in loose curls down her back. "I remember you used to always eat it in school. I figured even if you didn't eat it much anymore, you wouldn't mind it tonight." He picked up her plate and a glass and passed it to her. "Burrito and tacos, if I'm remembering right."

"I still eat it all the time, too much, actually." She took the plate from his hand and smiled. "I can't believe you saw me in my mask."

"You didn't have to wash it off." He picked up his plate and glass. "You looked fine."

"Liar. Come on. Let's go eat on the couch."

Drake followed her into the living room and sat on one corner of the light gray tweed sofa. Esther sat on the other corner and pulled her legs in, bending her knees and crossing them in front of her. She didn't look mad. That was good. "Do you want to say the blessing, or I can?"

"You can." Esther leaned forward and set her glass on the glass top coffee table. "Okay."

Drake set down his cup and stretched his arm across, reaching for her hand. She slipped her warm hand into his, and a jolt stirred in his chest. He cleared his throat, then bowed his head. "Lord, thank you for this food. Thank you for our friendship. Thank you for not letting me fall out of that oak tree and break my neck. Amen."

"Amen." Esther slipped her hand from his. "Sorry about not letting you in."

"Sorry about breaking in through Barlow's window. That's how we used to sneak out when we were in school."

"You did it more than once?" Esther's brow wrinkled. "I thought that only happened once, and Papaw caught you."

"No." Drake grinned. "We learned to leave the window up a crack so he wouldn't hear it squeak when we first lifted it. We snuck out all the time. Pretty much every time I came over. We walked down to the store on the corner and hung out, thinking we were bad."

Esther twisted her lips to the side. "You quit spending the night when you moved out to where you are living now, so you two must have been in what, sixth or seventh grade?"

"Dad got sick when I was in sixth grade, and we had to

move in seventh. To sixth graders walking to the gas station after dark when you're supposed to be in bed is big stuff."

Esther unwrapped her burrito and inspected the end. "Do you own all of that land out at your mother's place now?" She took a bite, and a string of lettuce stuck to her chin.

Drake handed her a napkin. "Momma got a settlement from a lawsuit dealing with Daddy's lung cancer and asbestos from that old closed down factory. It wasn't much, but she bought the little house I'm in and the ten acres around it. I bought the house and a couple of acres from her back when I was doing construction. She moved out so Paige and I could have the place to ourselves. She bought her trailer with the money." Drake unwrapped one of his tacos and laid it back on his plate. "Look. I need to talk to you about something."

"It's alright, Drake." Esther leaned forward and picked up her glass. "I got mad and spouted off. Your business is your business."

"No." Drake reached over and touched her hand. Her eyes looked up into his. A tightness started in his gut, and he pulled his hand back. He needed to say what he had to say. Why was touching her hand so distracting? "You were right—about everything. After Gracie was born, the doctor warned Paige that she didn't need to have any more kids. Her blood sugars had messed up with Gracie, but they got back okay when she was born. I wanted another boy so Scout could have a brother, you know, like me and Quinn."

"So." Esther's eyes softened. "She got pregnant again."

"Yeah, for me. I figured she was young and one more pregnancy wouldn't hurt, but, as you know... it did."

"Drake." Esther set her plate on the table and unfolded her legs, scooting to the middle of the sofa. "What happened to Paige was not your fault."

"In a way it was, Esther." Drake swallowed. "But it's okay. I've made peace with it. I know where Paige is now, and I know God doesn't hold what happened to her against me. Lord knows I would never have asked her to try again if I'd known what was in store."

Esther reached her hand out and laid it on Drake's. "I can't imagine how hard it must have been."

"It was pretty bad for a while. I honestly don't know what I would have done without Momma and Quinn and Hank. The church folks were good to me, heaven knows, but when I needed help in the middle of the night with squalling young'uns, family is who I called."

"I'm sure your mother didn't mind being there for you, and you know your brothers will do anything for you."

"The thing is." Drake took his plate from his lap and set it on the coffee table by Esther's, never pulling his hand from hers. "When your grandma and your uncles help raise you, and you're the baby who happens to look just like your deceased mother but has a mean streak like your daddy, things can get a little out of control."

"She's a sweet girl. She's just very strong willed."

"Yeah, but I've been letting her get away with murder."

"Yes. I believe you have." Esther's lips pushed up in a smile. "That's not good for her."

"I know. I had a long talk with the kids. I'm going to do better."

"Good."

Drake reached his other hand over and took Esther's hand in his. "Will you come back? The kids want you to start hanging out with us again."

"The kids?"

"The kids." Drake looked down at Esther's hand, then back up at her face, searching his. "And me."

Chapter Twelve

Esther looked around the park at all the children toting their baskets and running in one direction or the other. Toddlers walked with one parent beside them, sometimes two, pointing to the brightly colored eggs nestled in the green grass all scattered at their feet. The annual Carson's Bayou town wide egg hunt was scheduled every year on the Saturday before Easter. It was probably the only hunt in the country where a person in the normal bunny suit hid the eggs for the small ones, but their own infamous Carson Gator hid the eggs for the older kids.

Esther looked across the park where Sidney Madison, the oil change guy from across town, towered over the children in the green costume, complete with a pointy snout and sweeping spikey tail. Sidney was a member of the bigger church in town, and Esther didn't really know him that well. He had been older than her in school but had always kept a reputation for being a quiet guy. It seemed odd since Carson Gator was strolling among the school-age kids, trying to sneak eggs from their baskets in a very outgoing sort of way.

Molly, with Drake a few paces behind, darted from one

place to the other, greedily harvesting and hoarding the Easter eggs. "Daddy, I'm going to the big kid hunt this year. You don't need to follow me around."

Drake had insisted he needed to be there with his youngest, and after a long debate ending in an ultimatum of him going or her staying up the hill at the bunny hunt, Molly finally caved. Drake was not concerned about Molly's safety down the hill with the older kids. He wasn't concerned about her not being able to keep up with the older children and being disappointed with an empty basket at the end of the hunt. No, Molly being Molly, he was more concerned about her resorting to nefarious hunting techniques to fill her basket.

"You forget," Esther said, laughing at Drake rolling his eyes at his youngest daughter as they drove to the park earlier that day, ice chest and picnic basket secured in the back of the truck. "I hunted eggs with you and your brothers at this hunt as a kid. I believe you are the very reason that Carson Gator and Billy Bunny read off the list of rules before every egg hunt begins."

"Really, Daddy?" Scout leaned forward from the backseat of the truck. "There was an Easter egg hunt when you were a boy?"

"Sure was." Drake had smiled as he turned into the entrance to the city park, already overflowing with townsfolk who were getting ready for the event put on by all the local Carson's Bayou churches. "Me and your uncles won the golden egg three years in a row."

"Whoa," Molly said, her eyes round with hero worship. "Scout, when they count the eggs, you and Gracie put all your eggs in my basket so I can win the gold egg today."

"That's against the rules," Esther said, glancing over her shoulder as she unbuckled her seatbelt. "If Carson Gator catches you cheating like that, ask your dad what happens."

The three children all turned their eyes to their father. He turned off the truck and twisted around in his seat. "He tapes a big black egg on your back. Him and Billy Bunny don't count your eggs in the contest at all. You get marked as a bad egg."

The kids had hurried ahead to turn their eggs in at the egg gathering station and get ready for the hunt. Drake and Esther gathered the picnic supplies from the back of the truck. "If the preachers hadn't wrangled me, Quinn, and Hank in on that third year, we would have controlled the biggest egg mafia business in the parish," Drake said, passing the quilt over to Esther.

"I'm glad you left that little bit of knowledge out of your story," Esther said, watching Drake lift the large red ice chest with wheels and a pull handle to the ground. "Molly's little apple falls too close to your tree. I'm afraid a second generation of Lewis strong armed egg gathering tactics might shed a poor light on the family name."

"I agree."

Esther's lips tilted up in the corners at the memory. She watched a young mother kneel by her son and pick up his fake grass and the two eggs he had dumped out of the basket in his eagerness to hunt. The child, with his beautiful olive skin and gentle round eyes, was the spitting image of the woman beside him. Esther's smile faded. The longing, the one that was near and dear to her, reared its head. Would her children favor her like that, or would they look more like Drake? Maybe they would have a mash-up. His color hair and eyes and her curls and complexion. *So, I'm already having Drake's children now?*

A little gust of wind blew a leaf across the grass and onto the corner of the quilt. Esther leaned forward and brushed it off. She breathed in. Someone nearby was grilling burgers. Drake's deep laughter floated up the hill mixing with all the chatter and happiness around her. *I've loved him for so long.* Even when she found out he married Paige, and her mind gave up hope, her heart had held on. She always noticed when Drake was anywhere remotely in her presence. For him, it had only been three weeks, a new relationship starting when he came to her house and asked her to give him and the kids a chance. For her—it had been a lifetime.

Since that Saturday, they had been together every chance they could. Drake never actually said they were dating, and true, the kids were always with them, but surely... She gnawed her lower lip, scanning the crowd down the way near the duck pond for Drake and Molly. Surely, after the way he came to her house, said he needed her back, he meant *him,* Drake the man, not Drake the father. *He can't separate the two, can he? Am I jumping to conclusions? I'd better talk to him and find out where this is going instead of drifting along like a bubble in a hailstorm.*

"Miss Esther," Scout asked, walking up to the side of the blanket. "Can I have a juice box? Daddy said to come ask you?"

"Of course you can." Esther raised up on her knees and fished the drink from the ice chest, handing it to the boy. Scout jogged back down the gently sloping hill to where the other kids his age were, holding his basket away from his body so he didn't dump out any eggs. *I've got to talk to him, if not for my own peace of mind, then for the kids. Am I a friend, their free nanny service, or their future mother?* Esther pushed her sunshades back on her head and looked up at a gray cloud creeping into the horizon. *I've got to talk to Drake.*

Drake pulled into his driveway and looked in his rearview

mirror. Molly's head lay over on Gracie's shoulder, her eyes closed. Gracie's and Scout's heads were both bent back against the truck seat, mouths open, slumbering away. "They are worn out."

"I'll get Molly." Esther unbuckled her seatbelt and turned, looking behind her. Drake killed the truck engine and Scout's eyes fluttered open, but closed again. "Do you want me to lay her on her bed?"

"Yeah." Drake opened his truck door and leaned the seat forward. "Just slip her shoes off. I'll let her nap an hour and that will give me time to get supper together." He reached across Scout and unbuckled Gracie's seatbelt. "You are staying for supper, aren't you?"

"I'm not sure, but I do need to talk to you about something while we are alone."

"Okay." Drake picked up Gracie, her head flopping against his shoulder, and stood up in the late afternoon sun. He watched Esther walk across his yard and disappear through the screen door into his house. Something had been off when he got back to the blanket after helping Molly hunt eggs. Esther wasn't acting mad. She was being nice, laughing with the kids, and getting along fine with him, but she was... reserved. That was it.

He toted Gracie into her bedroom and passed Esther heading to the kitchen. For the next several minutes, he busied himself toting in Scout, the ice chest, picnic basket, and the other things. Esther fixed them a glass of tea and waited on the back porch.

"Thank you." Twenty minutes later, he took the sweaty glass from Esther's hand and sat down on the steps beside her. "I smell rain," he said. The deep pink sunset with streaks of purple glowed in the western sky in front of them. "I need to get them towels off the line in a minute."

"Drake." Esther stared out at the painted sky. "Where are we going?"

Drake set the glass on the step between his worn cowboy boots. *Ah, that's what it is.* "What do you mean?" He scooted his hips over and turned to face Esther. "Like over the next few years, or months, or just in general?"

"I mean." Esther turned, staring at Drake's face. "I need to know if you are keeping company with me because you want to as... a man, or just as a father."

"Esther." Drake looked into her eyes, her feelings pouring from them, demanding an answer. "I have feelings for you. Feelings that I didn't even realize I was capable of having anymore until the day I climbed into your window. I thought all of that died. With Paige."

A new look, not the timid look of worry that had been there until this point, crept onto Esther's face. Her tongue ran across her lips. "I need to tell you something."

Drake's hand came up of its own accord and stroked his fingers across Esther's cheek. "Okay," he whispered, his gut tingling with a warmth and softness.

"I love you."

Esther leaned forward, and Drake's hand moved from her cheek to the back of her neck, pulling her toward his lips. He leaned down and captured her lips with his. The kiss drew him in. The rest of the world vanished. There was only Esther... sweet Esther who had been in the background of his life since he was a child, now beside him, telling him she loved him.

"Drake." Esther's hand pushed against his shoulders, and she pulled back. "Did you hear what I said?"

"I did." Drake pulled in a deep breath and dropped his hands to his side. "I didn't mean to do that." He leaned back against the step railing and ran his hand along his jawline. "I'm falling for you, Esther. That wasn't my intention when we started out. I've figured I would never go." He ran both of his hands through the top of his hair and stretched his shoulders back, clearing his thoughts. "I figured I would be alone for the rest of my life."

"I did too, but Drake." Esther reached up and touched his arm.

A ripple of something intense from her simple touch pushed to the surface. Drake swallowed the lump growing in his throat. "Yeah," he whispered, staring at Esther.

"I've always loved you. Don't say anything. I know it's kind of pitiful, but it's true. Ever since we were kids—it's always been you."

"I had no idea, Esther." Drake's eyes opened wide. He stared at her, then looked away. "Why didn't you say something... before you left for college?"

"You were Barlow's best friend. I'm Barlow's twin sister. Back then, we were sort of a package deal." Esther paused, and Drake's gaze turned back to her face. "I didn't think you would take me seriously."

"I don't imagine it would have gone over too well with Barlow." Drake's eyes narrowed, or Quinn for that matter. "He had a crush on you there for a while until Barlow threatened to beat him within an inch of his life if he acted on it."

"See what I mean?" A faint smile crept onto Esther's face. "I figured you and I would never happen, so I kept everything to myself."

"And when you came back, I was married to Paige."

"Yes." Esther leaned back against the steps behind her. "I went out with a few guys every once in a while, but nobody was ever... you."

Drake stared at Esther, her words crashing into his brain. Growing up as a kid, the Sartins had always been his wealthy friends. Not that they acted any differently or made him or his brothers feel any less than them. The opposite was true.

His mother; however, never let him or his brothers forget that the Lewis boys worked and earned everything they got. All Barlow Sartin had to do was ask his father for a vehicle or a college education or whatever, and his wealthy daddy made sure it happened. He had assumed Esther always considered him and Quinn and Hank out of her league, beneath her. That idea had been drilled into him, and he believed it.

Until after he married Paige, after he got saved, his mother's views had colored a lot of his thinking in stormy, judgmental shades of gray. Even now, since Esther was coming over and they had started hanging out, those same feelings... him being a hardware store manager with no college education and her being a nurse practitioner... they had pushed forward. "What do we do now?" Drake looked over at Esther, her eyes staring at his face.

"We date." Esther smiled. "That is, if either of us remembers how."

Chapter Thirteen

"We could have just grabbed a burger somewhere," Esther said, looking around at the couples sitting at nearby tables covered in white linen cloths with small candles flickering in the center. "We didn't need to leave Carson's Bayou."

"I know, but since we decided to do this, I figured we might as well do it right." Drake, wearing one of two white dress shirts that hung in the closet untouched for literally years at a time, and new dark wash jeans his children insisted he get for the occasion when they were in Target earlier that day, glanced around the steakhouse. "With Paige, we were both so young and so broke that our dates were a trip to Taco Bell and then a park bench, which was fine. I can do a little better now, and I want to, at least every once in a while."

"Well, I appreciate all the effort you put into this. This is nice."

Esther smiled across at Drake in the dim light, and his heart did a little gallop. "Esther." Drake slipped his hand across the table, reaching for hers. "I know we got off to a, well... an awkward start. My situation with the kids and working two jobs and having my family so involved in every part of my life is not ideal, but..."

"Drake." Esther reached up and put her hand on top of his. "I love your kids. I love you. That's all that matters. I can't imagine you without them. I respect the way you do whatever it takes to provide for them and still manage to be around when they need you."

"I just don't want you to, well, regret getting involved with me."

"That's never going to happen."

The waiter walked up and placed water glasses on their table and took their drink orders. Drake studied Esther as she smiled up at the young man handing her the menu. How did he get so blessed? It was like he was waking up from living in a dark gray fog, like he was starting to live life again, not just exist. "Molly is doing so much better since you..." Drake paused and slipped his hand into his jeans pocket. He grabbed his vibrating phone as the waiter walked off. "It's Quinn," he said, looking at the screen. "Hello."

"Daddy."

"Scout. What's wrong? Where's Uncle Quinn?"

"He's outside with Gracie and Molly petting Poochie. He said Poochie is gonna be a momma real soon."

"Okay, son." Drake looked across the table at Esther's concerned face. "It's fine," he mouthed silently as his son rattled on about Poochie's upcoming litter of puppies. "Scout, why did you call me?"

"Daddy, can I stay up until you get home? I don't go to school or church tomorrow."

"Ask Uncle Quinn. Whatever he says is fine with me." Drake said, keeping the irritation from his voice. "Goodbye."

The waiter walked back up with their teas, and they placed their orders. Drake ordered steak and grilled shrimp, Esther a ribeye. "What I was going to say before the call,"

Drake said, "is that Molly is doing a lot better with the temper tantrums since you have started visiting." He paused again and slipped his hands back into his pocket. "Hold on." He looked at the vibrating phone. "I wouldn't answer it, but if I don't, something will be wrong."

"No, you need to answer it," Esther said, smiling, a glimmer of amusement in her eyes. "It's kind of entertaining."

"Daddy."

"Yes, Gracie."

"Molly got the butter out and is rubbing it on her legs and letting Rambler lick it off."

"Let me talk to Uncle Quinn." Drake's jaw clenched, but his voice was calm. "Put him on the phone, honey."

"He's in the bathroom with the door locked."

Drake ran his fingers through the top of his hair. "Let me talk to Molly." He listened as Gracie screamed for Molly to come inside and get the phone.

"Daddy." Molly's voice finally came over the phone several minutes later. "I love you. I hope you are having a good time."

"Molly, did you put butter on your legs?" Drake looked across the table where Esther was suppressing a chuckle. Momma had refused to babysit the kids tonight. Quinn had stepped in and taken them. Momma was being her usual self, but Esther didn't need to hear that.

"The last thing you need to be doing is going out with that uppity Sartin woman," his mother had said when he had asked her to watch the kids. "I'm not having any part of you getting your heart broken." He ended up bribing Quinn into looking after them by agreeing to put the skirting up around his trailer while he was away on his next oil field hitch. No, Esther didn't need to know all that.

"Molly, Gracie said you rubbed butter on your legs, and you know Gracie doesn't lie."

"Well."

A crash reverberated through the phone, and Drake pulled it away from his ear until it was quiet again. "Molly?"

"I dropped the phone. My hands are slippery."

"Molly. Did you get in the butter?"

"Yes, but it's not on my legs now. Rambler and Poochie licked it off."

"Go put the butter up and..."

"I can't."

"Why not?"

"It's all gone."

"Molly. I'm going to hang up now. Go give Scout the phone and don't do anything you know I won't let you do." Drake waited for an answer. "Molly?" Grunting and breathing came from the phone. "Molly?"

"Yes, Daddy?"

"Did you hear me?"

"Daddy, did you know that I can go under the house if I slide on my belly?"

"Molly, where are you?"

"Bye, Daddy."

Drake looked at the screen. "She hung up on me." He hit redial and called Quinn's number back. "Molly's climbing under the house. As warm as it is, there's liable to be snakes under there."

"Where's Quinn?" Esther asked, setting down her tea glass. "Drake, snake bites can be deadly to kids as small as Molly."

"According to Gracie, he's locked himself in the bathroom." Drake pushed the ringing phone tightly to his ear. "Nobody's answering."

Esther stood up and tossed her linen napkin on the table. "Come on."

"We don't have to go," Drake said, standing as the words came out of his mouth. "Quinn will probably call back in a minute." He pulled his wallet out and threw twenty dollars on the table. Esther was right. He couldn't sit here and eat and act like nothing was happening at home. One thing was certain, though. Quinn Lewis would not be getting skirting around his trailer next week.

"I went to the bathroom, Drake," Quinn snapped. "Believe it or not, I need to do that sometimes."

"Why did you lock the door?" Drake stared at his little brother in the dim moonlight as they sat on the front porch steps. Esther was inside, giving Molly a bath to wash off all the dust and grime from her crawl under the house. "Scout could have handed you the phone if you'd left the door unlocked."

"Unlike you, I prefer to take care of my business without three sets of eyes staring at me." He leaned over and scratched Rambler behind the ears. "Besides, everything was fine. You didn't have to come home. I had them under control."

"Molly was under the house, Scout was watching a zombie movie, and Gracie was meddling in my closet."

"What's your point?" Quinn grinned at his brother. "They're still breathing."

"It's not funny." Drake's eyes narrowed. "You know snakes are crawling this time of year. What if a ground rattler or a copperhead had been under the house and bitten Molly?"

"Snakes aren't no match for your little spitfire." Quinn continued to smile, his white teeth shining in the moonlight. "Chill out, man. Everybody's fine. You jumped the gun and run home when there wasn't no need. That's on you, not me."

"Everything okay out here?" Esther stepped through the

screen door and looked at the brothers. "You might want to keep it down. I just put the kids in bed."

"See there, Big Brother?" Quinn stood up and stretched his arms above his head. "No harm, no foul." He looked down at the dog, still lying at his feet. "Come on, Rambler. We better head across the road before we wear out our welcome."

Drake watched Quinn's shadowy figure disappear across the gravel road into the darkness. "I should have known better than to get him to keep them."

"Nobody was hurt," Esther said, sitting down on the step beside Drake. "Did you find his phone?"

"No. He's going to look under the house again tomorrow when it's daylight." Drake draped his arm around Esther's shoulders. "I hope it doesn't go to ringing in the middle of the night. Molly crawled right under my bedroom."

Esther leaned her head over on Drake's shoulder. "I must say that this is the most interesting first date I've ever been on."

"Well, I'm going to make sure that the second date is a nice, normal, boring night out. No snake scares, no buttered down young'uns, no pregnant Poochie."

"Now, what's the fun in that?" Esther put her hand over her mouth as a yawn crept out. "What was that you were telling me before we left the restaurant? How Molly is doing so much better?"

"Yeah," Drake chuckled. "A lot better. The way I figure it, though, I'm on the home stretch. If I can hang in there a couple or three more years, my kids will all be big enough that I can at least leave them alone for five minutes without worrying about them burning the house down or something else as crazy."

"But by that time, hopefully we will have tied the knot and there'll be another one on the way," Esther said, raising her head. "Then we will be going through all of this together, so it won't be so bad."

"Oh, no." Drake shook his head. "We aren't going through that. I'm all for tying the knot when the time is right, but once we get these three under control, I'm not going down that path again."

Esther leaned away from Drake, staring into his face in the darkness. "Drake, you aren't serious."

"I am." Drake smiled down at Esther. "The last thing I want to do is raise more kids. Don't get me wrong, I love those three, but you have no idea how hard it is being a parent."

"I guess..." Esther reached up and lifted Drake's arm from around her shoulder. "I always assumed you understood that I wanted to have a child."

"You *will* have a child," Drake said, his brow drawing low. "You'll have three of them. Don't worry. You'll have so much to do with those three that you won't even have time to worry about having another one."

"You know I love them." Esther slapped a mosquito on her arm. "That's not the point. The point is, I want to get pregnant and have a baby... our baby, Drake."

"Why are we even talking about this now?" Drake let out a tense chuckle. "We haven't even gone out on our first date yet, and we're already talking about marriage and kids."

Esther stood and took a step into the darkness.

"Hey." Drake stood up. "Where are you going? We can go in and make grilled cheese and find an old movie to watch."

"No." Esther turned, and Drake strained his eyes to read her expression in the faint light. "I'm going home, Drake. I need to think about all this."

"All what, Esther?" Drake stepped toward her, but Esther held her hand up. "Don't be like this. Come on in and let's talk this through. Once I explain it all to you, you'll see that I'm right."

"I need to go home. I'll see you... later."

Drake watched Esther climb into her vehicle and disappear down the gravel road. More kids? Why were they even discussing more kids? He sat back down and leaned his head against the porch post. *She doesn't know what it's like worrying about a sickly kid, crying all the time, wanting its mother and not being able to soothe it.* He massaged his fingers against his temples. He couldn't go through that again. One wife had died because he wanted a child. No, if Esther got pregnant and something happened to her....

Drake pulled in a deep breath of air and stared into the inky night. Esther would come around to his way of thinking. He just needed to give her time.

"Should Have Been A Cowboy" rang out from somewhere under the porch. Quinn's phone was definitely not on silent. It was going to be a long night.

Chapter Fourteen

The cool antique doorknob pushed against Esther's palm. She unlocked the door, sending a wave of familiar comfort through her being. How many times had she come in this front door after dark... alone? How many times would she do it again? *How can we be so connected but still be so out of sync with something so important? Are we in sync?* Her purse thudded on the table in the foyer as she continued to the living room. *Am I fooling myself? I've wanted this so badly for so long.*

She fell into the recliner in the darkness, not bothering to reach over and turn on the light. She wanted to process what had happened tonight, what had happened since February. That could happen without the light. Had they ever talked about having kids, more kids, her kids, before? She searched her memories. They had been together so much and talked about kids and family all the time. Pictures of them. She and Drake and the kids rolled through her thoughts. Them at the park, at the grocery store, in their backyard, at the church, going fishing at the pond down the trail behind Drake's house all played through her head, mixing with the rare occasion when it was just her and Drake alone.

No, ever since she told him she loved him, which now seemed like decades ago, even though it had only been a week, they had fallen into a new routine. She would go by his house after work and spend the evening with them before coming home. It had been like slipping on an old familiar glove. Like she fit there, she belonged there, like Drake wanted what she wanted and felt the way she did. *He's never actually said he loves me.*

Her phone vibrated, and she pulled it from her skirt pocket, the lighted screen glowing in the darkness.

> I'm sorry our night ended the way it did. I'll do better next time.

She stared at the screen. Was what she wanted so badly, so deep inside her coloring her reality of what was going on, of what Drake wanted from their relationship?

> Okay.

Possibly, at least a little. Even so, he had come to her when she pushed him away. That had to mean something.

> Talk tomorrow?

> Yes.

She dropped the phone beside her and laid her head back on the couch, staring into the darkness. They had to talk. Really talk, alone without the kids, without the cell phones to distract them. *I have to know how he feels, where he stands.* A ripple of fear ran down her back. What if he didn't love her? No, Drake was a good man. He was not a person who would lead her on or take advantage of what she had shared with him... her heart.

He might have feelings for me—love me, but not as much as I love him. Esther scooted her hips over and curled on to her side. She pulled the afghan Granny had crocheted decades ago from the back of the recliner and stretched it across her legs. Barlow insisted on keeping the house goosebumps cold no matter what the temperature was outside, but he paid the electric bill, so she suffered in silence.

The big question was, could she settle for loving Drake on his terms? Would a life with Drake and the kids be enough? Could she give up her plans of becoming pregnant and having children with him?

Her hand pressed against her stomach. *What's my alternative? Do I want to spend the rest of my life sitting on the couch pining away for him? Not the real him, but the him I've built up in my mind?* Her stomach rumbled, but food was the last thing she wanted. Her phone buzzed again, and she raised her head and glanced at the text from her mother.

> Hey, honey, your grandmother told me you are dating Drake Lewis. We haven't chatted in a while. Would love for you to drive down for a visit. Perhaps a long weekend? The beach is beautiful. What do you think?

Great. Everybody knows I'm seeing Drake. What did I expect? Their town was small, and Drake had been by the Children's Clinic several times to bring her lunch. No wonder the gossip had made its way to Granny's assisted living.

How long had it been since she had gone to see her parents? Last fall. She had been so consumed with Drake.

I might, Mom. Let me check my schedule and get back to you. Love you. Hug Dad for me.

The screen flashed again with a heart emoji.

She would talk to Drake tomorrow after church, insist they get alone somewhere, and really talk. She would listen, really listen to what he said... and what he didn't say. She reached down and dragged the afghan up over her shoulders, stretching her legs out across the recliner in front of her. Where was Barlow? Had she locked the front door? A wave of fatigue washed over her, and she rolled over as her eyes drifted shut. She would get up and go to bed later, when Barlow came in, after a little nap.

Esther massaged her aching neck with the tips of her fingers, a product of spending the night on her recliner instead of her bed. Barlow had picked up an extra shift at the hospital last night and woke her up when he came in at seven thirty that morning. Now, sitting on the church pew waiting for Sunday school to be over, she regretted never getting up and going to where she would have slept better. The last thing she needed today was to be half asleep and grouchy.

"Miss Esther." Gracie slipped into the pew beside Esther and pulled her out of her pity party. "Guess what we are doing after church?"

Esther wrapped her arm around the girl's slim shoulders and gave her a squeeze as she climbed up on the pew. "Let's see. Home to eat a hotdog."

"Wrong." Gracie's eyes sparkled with enthusiasm.

"Mawmaw and Mr. Howard are taking us to the pond to go fishing. I like to fish, but I don't touch the worms. Mawmaw said Mr. Howard will help me bait my hook."

"That sounds like a fun afternoon." Esther's eyes scanned the sanctuary as people started coming in from the side doors. Sunday school must have let out. She would have to try to talk to Drake this evening after his fishing trip.

"I asked Daddy if you wanted to come, but he said you and him were doing something else today."

Esther looked back down at the child. "Your dad isn't going fishing?"

"No, ma'am, but if you want to go, we can ask him for you." Gracie pushed her bangs from her eyes. "It's going to be a lot of fun."

"Thank you, sweetie." Esther brushed back the girl's silky, straight hair as it fell across her eyes again. It was time to take all three kids back to get their hair cut. "I think I'll pass today, but I definitely want to go again one day."

Esther looked up as Drake and Molly came through one of the side doors holding hands. Molly was talking, her forehead creased, and a stern look on her face. Drake was nodding his head, but his eyes were scanning the pews. Esther waited until they stopped on her, then pushed her lips into a timid smile. After all the turmoil from last night, wondering if she was seeing things in this relationship that weren't really there, she felt like she was standing on quicksand.

Drake and Molly stepped up to the end of the pew and slid in. Drake shooed Molly and Gracie to the other side of Esther, and he sat between the end of the seat next to her. "Are you busy after church? I thought you and I could grab a bite to eat and talk."

"That would be good," Esther said, again forcing herself to smile. Drake stretched his arm behind her along the back of the pew. Esther's body longed to snuggle into the crook of his arm, but she sat straight, not giving in to the urge. The seats were filling up, and the piano started playing. Scout and a couple of other boys his size slid into the pew in front of Esther and Drake, just as the song director asked everyone to stand for the opening prayer.

Lord, guide me in what to do today. I want to give up on my desire to have a child, if that's what it takes to be Drake's wife. I'm afraid if I do, though, I will resent him later for forcing this decision on me. I don't want to be like that. Help me decide what to do.

DRAKE PULLED up at the Gumbo Hut and searched for Esther's car. He offered to drop by and pick her up after he got the kids settled with his mother and Harold, her long-standing friend who she refused to call her boyfriend. Esther said she would take her own car and meet him there. Hopefully, she would be back to her normal happy, easy-going self. At church she had been standoffish.

Drake weaved through the vehicles in the packed parking lot and made his way inside the little restaurant. People sat in chairs along the wall next to the entrance waiting for their called in orders. The place buzzed with the usual Sunday lunch crowd. The aroma of fried hushpuppies and seafood reached his nose and his stomach growled.

"Esther's in the back corner." A tall skinny waitress with blue gray hair pulled back in a ponytail pointed to the far wall. "What you want to drink? Esther's having a Coke."

"A Coke is fine." Drake thanked the waitress. She also worked at the gas station near the school. Her name was Carol something, he couldn't remember. He weaved between the tables humming with conversation to where Esther waited. "This place is slamming," he said, looking down at her face.

"It is." Esther looked up and smiled the same smile he saw at church.

Drake sat down across from her. The waitress stepped up to their table and plopped down two enormous red plastic tumblers full of soda. She took their orders and weaved her way back through the crowded room to the kitchen.

Drake looked at Esther, busying herself with pulling the paper off her straw. "Esther, what's wrong? I can tell you're upset with me. Is it what I said about more kids?"

Esther's eyes looked up at Drake, her face a mixture of dread and determination. "Drake, you know how I feel about you. I told you." She stuck the straw into the glass and slowly stirred around the crushed ice. "Am I wasting my time?"

"No." Drake's eyebrows shot up. "What would make you say something like that?"

"You've never said." Esther pushed her lips together, her eyes darting around at the people, the happy families chatting away nearby. She looked back at Drake's waiting face. "How do you feel about me? What do you see happening between us? If you just want a casual friend to hang out with you and your kids, then you and I are not on the same page at all."

"Esther, I don't kiss my casual friends." His eyes narrowed. Hadn't they already decided they were going to date? Where was this coming from? "I know we mostly hang out at my house or go run errands with the kids, but I really want to date you. That's why I asked you here today, to make up for the mess I made of things last night."

"How do you feel about me, Drake?" Esther reached her fingers up and rubbed her forehead. "I need you to tell me."

"I care for you, Esther. Deeply care. I just am not one to talk about this kind of stuff."

"You care for me." Esther's tone was flat, her mouth drooping. She pulled in a deep breath and let it out slowly. "Drake, I want to have a child with the person I marry."

"Esther…"

"Wait." Esther raised her hand. "Let me say this while I still can. I love your kids. I think you know that, but I want to have a child too. I've wanted to be a mother, have a baby ever since I was a little girl. It never entered my mind that I wouldn't have kids."

"I don't know if I can do that." Drake rested his elbow on the table and pushed his knuckles into his cheek. Why was she so caught up on this? "Seems like if you truly love me like you say you do, that I would be enough for you."

Esther's eyes narrowed, and her lips pulled into a straight line. "If I truly loved you? You won't even *say* you love me, but you'll throw my own words back in my face?"

"Esther, listen."

"No, Drake Lewis. You listen. I understand you have a lot on you raising your kids on your own, but I'm not asking you to do that for me. I'm asking you *if* we continue to see each other and *if* we decide to tie the knot, to *let* me have your child. And furthermore…" Esther leaned forward and threw her napkin on the table. "If you loved me, you would want to have children with me."

Drake sat up straight in the chair. "Look, Esther."

"Don't." Esther stood up, the chair rattling behind her. "I can't do this. I thought we wanted the same things, but you won't even say you love me, Drake."

"Esther be reasonable." Drake pulled his chair back and grabbed her arm, ignoring the stares from everyone in the place. "You dropped all this on me last week, and then last night you…"

"You're right." Esther pulled her arm away. "I thought this was something it wasn't. I'm sorry, truly sorry. Not for me or you. I'll get over you, and since your feelings aren't like mine, you won't have any trouble moving on. The kids, though. I never should have let myself get involved with your kids until I knew how you felt."

Drake stared at Esther, unsure what to say, what to do. She was asking too much of him too fast. "Maybe you're right. Maybe we moved too fast too soon."

A tear ran down Esther's face. "Goodbye, Drake."

Drake watched Esther weave through the tables and out the door.

"Man. Go after her."

Drake looked over at the old man in coveralls sitting alone at a nearby table. "It won't do any good. I can't give her what she's asking for."

Chapter Fifteen

"Daddy."

Drake let out a long sigh and rubbed his eyes. It had been two months since the breakup with Esther. The kids asked about her a lot for the first several days, but they gradually got back to their normal lives. There were a few rough patches, like when he came out of the bathroom one Saturday morning to find Gracie on his phone pouring her heart out to Esther about her worries over Poochie and the arrival of the puppies in the next few weeks. He had taken the phone from Gracie and apologized to Esther, but her voice, the way her words sort of melted together, punched him in the gut. She had been polite, and even cheerful, but after the initial chatting about the kids, the conversation lagged. What did you say to the woman that stole your heart? The one you let get away because she was asking for the one thing you couldn't give her?

"Daaa-ddyy." Scout drug the words out into a mournful sigh. Drake pushed up off the back-porch steps. He tossed the last swallow of coffee into the grass and looked out across the backyard. Scout had put on the washing last night while he did the dishes. This morning before dawn, he hung the load on the line. The dryer had gone out last year shortly after Thanksgiving. With Christmas coming up and things being lean over the holiday season with his repair man side hustle, he had put off making the big purchase. The truck had needed new brakes, and he had to get the kids a little something other than socks and underwear for Christmas. Like with all the other changes in their short lives, the kids had fussed about scratchy towels and stiff underwear from having to dry everything on the clothesline but had quickly rolled along.

"Dad?" Scout poked his head out the back door. "Can't you hear me?"

"Yeah, son, I was just saying my morning prayers and enjoying the sunrise." Drake smiled down at his son in his spaghetti stained t-shirt and pajama pants now well above his ankles. That one never complained about those kinds of things, always asking for things for his sisters instead of himself. "What's going on?"

"The water in the tub is cold. I tried turning it off and on, but it stays cold."

"Come on." Drake put his big, calloused hand on his son's head and pulled him against his leg. "That hot water heater is as old as the hills. The heating element is probably going out. I'll have to show you how to fix it."

They walked down the hall to the bathroom, and Drake looked at the floor. Water seeped out from under the closet door, soaking the bath rug and puddling at their feet. "That's not good." He opened the narrow door and squatted down, looking at the ancient hot water heater.

"There's water in my closet too," Scout said, squeezing in beside his daddy. "Worse than usual. I put a towel down."

"What do you mean worse than usual?" Drake stood up and turned to his son. "Your floor has been wet?"

"Yeah, Dad." Scout looked up at his father, his tone accusing. "Remember? I told you there was water down there a long time ago, and you told me to wipe it up and you would look at it."

Drake turned and stepped into the hall. He stuck his head into the girls' bedroom and looked at their sleeping forms. Gracie had left her bed and was cuddled up next to Molly, as was usual if Rambler hadn't snuck in to cuddle with her for the night. He pulled the bedroom door shut and stepped into Scout's room that shared a wall with the bathroom. He opened the closet door and looked down at the three soppy wet towels on the floor. Scout had moved everything else out to the folding chair in the corner of the room. He didn't remember Scout telling him about the water. There was so much to keep up with, so much to do and worry about. The split with Esther had only made things worse. He had been moping around in a haze, but he couldn't shake it, at least not for long, anyway.

Drake rubbed his hand along the back of his neck. "Go get a couple of Target bags and pick up these wet towels. Take them out back and spread them out on the rail to dry. It looks like there's a crack in the water heater tank."

"Can we fix it?" Scout rubbed the back of his neck and stepped back out of his daddy's way.

"Afraid not." Drake pulled in a huff of air and blew it out slowly. Even with his employee discount, a new water heater would cost more than he needed to spend at the moment.

"What y'all doing in here?" Quinn poked his head in the bedroom door, his usual grin in place. "I took the biscuits out of the oven before they burned when I came in."

"Thanks." Drake looked at his younger brother, still focused on the water heater. He could ask Quinn for the money, or Hank for that matter. Of course, he'd have to track Hank down. He hadn't been home since last summer. The last time he'd talked to him, his big brother was in North Dakota working on some kind of pipeline. Either brother would loan... give him the money for what he needed, no questions asked.

Quinn, for all his goofing around, was actually good with money. He lived in his trailer and was always bumming free labor off of Drake, but a few years back, he got interested in investing. Drake didn't know how much his little brother was worth, and wouldn't ask, but Quinn, being a confirmed bachelor, had opened up accounts for his nieces and nephew. He contributed to their college funds routinely—securing his kids' futures much more than Drake could, who always seemed to be scraping by.

No. He didn't want to go down that path. He already depended on Quinn too much, not monetarily, but in other ways. He didn't want to add his cash problems to the mix. "It's the water heater. What do you have planned for today?"

"I was thinking it would be a good day to install a hot water heater." Quinn patted his brother on the back as he walked past. "Cheer up, Big Brother. Me and Scout got your back." He winked down at Scout, who was grinning up at the uncle he idolized. "We'll have you scrubbing pots in water so hot it will burn your hide by the end of the day." Quinn trailed Drake up the hall and into the kitchen. "I saw Esther yesterday at the drugstore. She's lost some weight. and let me tell you, that girl is smoking hot, brother."

Drake stopped pouring his second cup of coffee and cut his eyes at his little brother. "She's going to get sick, losing weight like that. She needs to quit."

"I was thinking." Quinn stepped over to the cabinet and pulled out his usual mug with a picture of the old school Lou Ferrigno Hulk on the side. "Since you two are no longer..."

"Don't." The hair on the back of Drake's neck bristled, and he turned to his brother. "Just don't, Quinn."

"Alright, alright." Quinn picked up the coffeepot. "Never hurts to ask. I figured there was still something there, but since you shut it down." Scout squeezed in between the two men and Quinn let the words die. "Little pitcher, I forgot you were here."

"Can I have coffee-sugar-milk, Uncle Quinn, like you make when you watch us?"

"Sure can." Quinn pulled out another mug from the cabinet. "Us men will need plenty of coffee, biscuits, and bacon before we tackle dragging out that water heater and putting in a new one."

Drake half listened as Quinn and Scout chatted about what Scout had been doing at school the past week. Drake had seen Esther around town, too. He had taken to driving by her house in the evening when he got off work, through Taco Bell at lunch, even though he did not care for the place, and even driving by the Children's Clinic every once in a while... just to catch a glimpse. He saw her every Sunday at church, but it wasn't enough.

There was such a turmoil, a fight inside him that he couldn't win no matter how he reacted. If he went and talked to her, the longing to be with her about pushed him over the edge for the next several days. Sleepless nights with pictures of her face, imagining his rough hand on her soft cheek, ripped him up. If he stayed away, the ache and emptiness nearly drowned him. So... he had turned into a stalker, sneaking around, acting casual when he caught a glimpse of her during the week, dying a little inside when he didn't.

"Hey." Quinn threw a biscuit across the table and hit Drake in the face. "Snap out of it."

Drake picked the biscuit up from the table and set it on his plate. "What?"

"I said that you've got a birthday coming up next month. I

planned to get you a dryer, but I've changed my mind. Hot water is a better gift."

"No. I've got this." Drake reached to the middle of the table and got the homemade Mayhaw jelly Momma kept him supplied with. "Just help me get the old one out and the new one in."

"Whatever you say, boss."

They finished their breakfast about the time the girls came stumbling up the hall. Quinn fixed them a biscuit. Drake gathered a few saved milk jugs and ran them full at the tap, then walked out to the pump house and turned off the water. He called his momma and told her what was going on. She agreed to watch the girls and told him to drop off their laundry. She would take care of that for him too, while he worked on the water heater. Momma was a pain sometimes, manipulative most of the time, but she always came through in a pinch. In an hour, they were loaded up. Drake dropped the girls off to help Mawmaw pick blueberries, and the men headed to town.

"I know things are tight now," Quinn said, his voice low. He glanced over his shoulder at Scout, engrossed in a game on his dad's cell phone. "Why don't you let me at least loan you the money?"

"No, I don't want to start that." Drake gave his signal and turned into the hardware store, a mom and pop affair with two teen employees and him. "There'll always be something breaking or falling apart. I'll figure it out."

The men, two grown and one in the making, crossed the parking lot to the store where Drake spent so much of his time for so little pay. Would it really be any worse to go back to construction work and give the kids a decent home with decent clothes and decent food? If he did make a change, when he was away on a job, his momma would take care of them. He would only do jobs where he could come home at night, although it would be late. It might even work out better to find work where he could come home on the weekends. Then, when he was home, they wouldn't be so strapped for money. They could enjoy their time together instead of doing this kind of thing. Between the forty hours at the hardware store and all the time he spent scraping up handyman jobs, he was gone about that much anyway... almost.

About twenty minutes later, after looking at what the little store had to offer, he picked out the water heater that would do and pulled out the emergency credit card. If he didn't get it paid off in six months, the interest would eat his lunch. Yeah. Something had to change. The owner of the store gave instructions to the teen boy on which water heater to load up.

Drake leaned against the counter and looked out the big plate-glass window facing the street. Esther, thinner but still as beautiful as ever, strolled down the sidewalk... with a man. Drake straightened up from the counter and took a step forward, drawn to her, as always. She smiled at the man, laying her hand on his shoulder as they disappeared out of Drake's line of vision. He pulled in a deep breath.

"I tried to tell you, Big Brother." Quinn stepped up beside Drake and watched the couple pass out of view. "She is hot. I don't know who that guy is, but..."

"Enough, Quinn." Drake blinked, not looking at his brother. "Let's get home. I've got to get the water back on."

Chapter Sixteen

Esther wiped her brow with the back of her hand and turned up her water bottle. Summer had definitely arrived in Louisiana. Her legs, just starting to get a hint of a tan, stuck out from her gym shorts, and she poured a little of the water on each one. When she had gone to see the counselor after her meltdown, the lady had suggested Esther start walking every morning to help work out some of the stress and emotions she was not handling as well as she should. "Walk, Esther. Don't set a walking goal, or put pressure on yourself. Just walk, talk to God, enjoy nature, maybe listen to some uplifting music."

The first week of walking had ended the same every day. She would start out praying, counting her blessings, enjoying being outside, but then her mind would start its own journey. Her brain always ended up at the same place, at the feet of Drake Lewis, bawling like a baby. If the people around her noticed the woman strolling along with the earbuds in, squalling her eyes out, they were kind enough to ignore her and let her deal with her misery alone.

Finally... Finally, what the counselor was saying began to

seep into her heart and mind, helping her to heal. "You placed Drake in a position he was never meant to be in. For a relationship to work, the feelings have to be reciprocated, but there's a deeper issue here, Esther. There's only one who is perfect, who promises to never leave you or let you down, and can actually live up to that promise. You know that's Jesus. Until you put Him where He's supposed to be, you are never going to be who you need to be. Focus on this first."

The last tear drenched walk had been at twilight two weeks ago after work. Walking around the duck pond at the park, the tears flowing as usual, she had wandered off the jogging path and collapsed under one of the oaks. "Lord, forgive me. If Drake Lewis is not in the path you've laid before me, then I need to accept that." There was no audible voice, no bolt of lightning from the sky, just a reasoning inside her soul. *If I'm longing for a man that is not in God's plan for me, then I'm telling God that His plan is imperfect, and my plan is better. I'm saying God is not enough.*

"Oh Lord, forgive me. I've been so foolish." The bark of the oak tree pushing into her back prickled her body the same way her behavior of the past few weeks was now prickling her soul. "No more, Esther Sartin. You are enough in Christ."

Things had started to improve since then. She leaned back on the park bench and closed her eyes, enjoying the sound of the katydids singing in the summer sunset. Her appetite was slowly coming back, but she was trying to do better with her eating. Taco Bell six days a week for lunch was a heart attack waiting to happen.

She had never been much of a cook, but going through this gloomy time had brought about another good change that she was thankful for. Many evenings when Barlow was working and she was alone in their big family home, pining away for a man who didn't feel the same way, her grandparents had driven up with jambalaya, or something else equally as wonderful, in a pot big enough to feed an army. Her mother was behind this, no doubt, still caring for her even when she lived two states away.

"Esther, where are your groceries, your staples?" Granny had looked in her cabinets, the ones that had been hers years before. She had been appalled at the lack of food. Esther and Barlow didn't eat at home a lot. They worked and grabbed fast food or take out ninety percent of the time. "There's not enough in here to keep a cat alive. Spaghetti sauce and peanut butter?"

The next visit, Papaw toted in two armfuls of groceries. "Don't argue with your grandmother," he said when Esther followed them into the kitchen like a lost puppy. "When she gets her mind set on something the easiest thing to do is to go with the flow."

"You are what, thirty-five?'

"No, Granny, I'll be thirty next month."

"Close enough. It's time you learned to cook. All that schooling you got is good, but you need to learn how to feed yourself. Eleanor and I should have insisted you learned this back when you were younger instead of letting you chase after Barlow and his rowdy friends." Granny pulled her apron out of her monstrous purse and started tying it around her ample middle. "Get your apron on. Tonight, you are going to make chicken fried steak."

"I don't have an apron, Granny." Esther sat on the barstool as Papaw disappeared into the living room. "Honestly, Gran, you don't have to do this. I'm fine, really."

"No, you are not. You are wasting away to nothing. If your bottom lip drug any lower you would trip on it when you put your pants on." She started pulling groceries from the paper bags and setting them on the counter or putting them in the cabinet. "I miss all this storage space." She turned and looked over her shoulder at Esther. "What are you waiting for, child? Go get a towel to tie around you for tonight. I'll bring an apron for you next time. We've got supper to cook. Papaw turns into a bear if dinner is too late."

"Esther? Are you okay?"

Esther raised her head from the bench and opened her eyes. He'd lost weight too. That soft feeling, the one she used to long for, pushed into her chest. No, not today. She shoved it away. She would not go down that useless road again. "Hello, Drake."

"I saw you sitting here with your head back like that and was scared you were sick or something."

"No, just resting my eyes." She sat up straight on the bench and looked up at him, the sunset glowing behind him in shades of purple and blue. "It's so hot out, and I'm not in the best of shape. I just finished my walk around the pond."

"How've you been?" He stepped closer, shoving his hands in his jeans pockets. "You mind if I sit down?"

"No." Esther scooted to the other end of the short bench, giving him plenty of room. "Have a seat. I've been doing okay."

"You look... different. I see you at church, and around and I've been worried that you might have been under the weather. You've gotten sort of thin."

"No." Esther swallowed. "I'm making some changes." She nodded down at her gym shorts and water bottle. "I'm walking every day, eating less takeout. My coun... doctor said I needed to." She looked down at her hands then out across the pond. "I was a little, well." She swallowed again and looked over at Drake, staring at her. "I was messed up for a while and couldn't eat or sleep or anything, but..."

"Esther, I'm..."

"No." Esther held her hand up, stopping his words. "No, I'm fine now. I really am. I had turned you into this Prince

Charming in my mind. It was totally unfair to you and to me to expect you to be someone you weren't. I've... moved on."

"I'm still sorry." Drake reached his hand across the bench then pulled it back. "There are things I just can't handle right now."

"Drake." Esther pulled in a deep breath of air. "Really. I've moved on. I don't want to start this right now."

"Alright." Drake turned and faced her completely, his back against the corner of the bench. "I'm glad I ran into you. I wanted to tell you that I'm leaving."

"Leaving?" Esther's eyes jerked to Drake's face, still staring at her. *You sound desperate. Stop. Get a grip.* "Okay."

"Not permanently. I'm going offshore. I'm going to work the opposite hitch of Quinn until I can find something better. I've got to bring in more money, and right now that's the quickest way to do it."

"Oh." *Don't ask. This is not your concern.* "I suppose your mother is going to look after the kids while you're gone."

"Yeah. It's not ideal, but I don't know what else to do. That's why Quinn and I are doing opposite turn-arounds, so one of us will be there to help her all the time."

"That's... good."

"Quinn's not always the best role model, but he loves my kids."

Drake rubbed his hand across his face, and Esther stared, her eyes following his fingers across the dark whiskers along his jawline. "Are you growing a beard?"

"No." Drake's lips pushed up at the corners, a sad smile filling his face. "No, I haven't shaved. Friday was my last day at the hardware store. I guess I've kind of let myself go thinking about... everything."

"Tell your mother to call me if she needs help with the kids." Shadows crept around Drake's features as the sun eased away and twilight took its place. "You know, if Molly gets sick... or the others, of course."

"She's got it. I put it in her phone." Drake leaned forward, his hands on his knees. "I guess I better be getting home. I pull out in the morning. The kids are cooking a special supper. Momma's there, but I still need to make sure they don't burn the house down."

"That's nice."

"Do you want me to walk you to your car?" He stood and looked down at her through the oncoming darkness. "I'm parked right beside you."

"No. I'm going to sit here a minute." One of the park lights flickered on nearby, and the familiar low buzz of the bulb hummed in her ears. "Thanks though."

"I guess I'll see you at church when I get back in."

"Yeah."

Esther watched him turn and walk away, his steps slow. She put her fingers to her head and massaged her temples. Next time would be easier. It had to be. It hurt too much now. At least with him being out of Carson's Bayou half the time, she wouldn't be constantly scanning parking lots looking for him, finding him, wishing she hadn't found him because seeing him made things worse. She waved through the darkness as Lucas and Vivian Wade jogged by in the direction of the parking lot, Lucas pushing the jogging stroller with their little one inside.

The familiar sound of Drake's truck engine sounded through the evening, and Esther pushed herself up from the bench and grabbed her water bottle. Barlow was off this weekend. She had put pork chops in her new crock pot, another gift from Granny. The idea of food had lured a promise that he would be home by 7:30 this evening after his shift. He was probably already there. Hopefully he left her enough food to get her through until in the morning.

She made her way to her car and climbed behind the steering wheel. Of course, it didn't really matter. The idea of food after seeing *him* didn't have a lot of appeal. *I'm going to eat though. I will not go back there. Not today, not ever.* "We know that for those who love God all things work together for the good." Esther recited the verse as she started the car. "Show me the good, God. Help me see your plan in all this, not just my narrow vision."

Her phone buzzed, and she looked down at the text. A picture of Barlow and Papaw sitting at the bar eating dinner flashed on the screen.

Are you coming?

Or can we eat it all?

She smiled and pulled onto the road to her house. *I'm blessed.* The memory of Drake's face looking at her through the darkness tried to push back in. No, not today. *I'm stronger than I was. I will not go backwards, never again.*

Chapter Seventeen

"Momma, calm down. I'm sure she's close by." Drake shifted his phone to the other ear. The rain was coming down outside, but the worst of the storm had already moved inland. Working on Quinn's oil rig in the Gulf of Mexico had been an adjustment, mostly dealing with being away from the kids for a week at a time, but everyone had seemed to be getting used to this new life. Now; however, on his second hitch out, and halfway through his seven-day shift, Molly was missing. "Where's Quinn?" Drake listened as the wind howled outside on the derrick. "He's supposed to be helping you while I'm out. That's why we're working opposite weeks."

"He's out searching for her, Drake, but you've got to do something. We're under a tornado watch, and our baby is out there in it. I can't handle this."

Drake pushed his fingers to his forehead. "You're sure she's not at my house or over at Quinn's? Did you check in the shed? She's probably in there with Poochie and them puppies."

"Drake. Listen to me. She's gone. Molly is not here." Drake's mother's voice rose. "You've got to do something."

"Okay, Momma." He rubbed his fingers across his eyes. Momma was always melodramatic. If there was a real problem, Quinn would text or call him. "I'll talk to Quinn and get back to you. Keep looking for her. I'm sure she's fine."

Drake hung up his cell and punched in a text to his little brother.

> Momma called. Is she just doing her thing, or is something really wrong?

Drake sat down on the bed and stared around the room where the workers slept. Momma had called while he was eating breakfast, and he'd come back to his bunk to talk. His phone buzzed, and he looked down at his hands.

> Been looking for over an hour in all the usual places. Storm is bad. Calling for her, but the wind is loud. She probably can't hear me, and I couldn't hear her if she answered.

A sliver of panic ran down Drake's spine, and he stood from the bunk. One thing Quinn never did was overreact. Growing up with an overdramatic mother had made all three of the boys a little emotionally withdrawn, but Quinn was the worst, dealing with all situations with humor. This text didn't sound humorous at all.

> Do I need to come in early?

> Yes.

Drake's heart drummed in his chest, and his eyes darted around the room.

I'll get them to fly me in. Keep me updated.

She's only been missing an hour. She's okay. He rushed from the sleeping quarters to find his foreman. Requesting to be flown inland halfway through your hitch on your second week out would not sit well with his boss. He'd probably lose this job, but it didn't matter. Quinn's one-word answer spoke volumes. *My daughter is in danger, and I'm out here, miles away.*

All the valid reasons for leaving the kids floated out the window as he found the foreman and explained the situation. After talking to the pilot who checked the weather forecast, they scheduled a takeoff in thirty minutes. The flight inland would take an hour, then he had to drive home. He was at least four hours away from being able to do anything useful for his little girl. *God, why did I do this?* Drake squeezed his eyes shut as he gathered his things, begging the Lord to watch out over his child. *I didn't ask You about starting this job. I just decided to do this and did it.* The realization slammed into his head as he zipped his duffle bag. *God, I'm sorry. I know I left my kids for others to care for without even seeking your counsel, but please, God...*

Drake sank to the bunk, his head buried in his hands. He'd lost his wife and somehow survived. No, not somehow. He'd leaned on the Lord, and He'd brought him through. "Lord. I put Molly in your hands. You know my intentions were good when I took this job, but I should have called on you with my troubles instead of doing things my own way. I see now." Drake stopped and pulled in a shuddering breath. *Why did I ever think leaving them was the right thing to do?* "I see that leaving my children to be cared for by people who are lost, even if they are family, is not what's best for them. God, I know this is not punishment from You, because you promise good for the ones who love you... and I love you God. Please keep my girl from harm."

Esther stared at the computer screen, looking over the lab work of one of her young diabetic patients. Normally in the afternoon the clinic was as busy as a beehive, but with the storm blowing through, and the tornado watch on until six that evening, almost everyone had called and rescheduled. She was using the time to review lab work and make follow-up phone calls.

She picked up the Mountain Dew bottle near the computer screen and drained the last few drops. She had done better with a lot of her bad habits, like living on Taco Bell and eating ice cream for supper, but giving up Mountain Dew was a completely different thing. Her cell phone vibrated in her scrub pocket. She pulled it out and looked at the number. Drake's mother? Drake had texted her the number before he went offshore, so if his mother did happen to call her, Esther would not think it was spam and ignore the call.

"Hello."

"Miss Esther?"

"Scout?" The child's voice sounded stressed. "Is everything okay? Did the school let out early because of the weather?"

"Yes, ma'am."

Esther listened, but the child didn't speak. "Scout? What's wrong? You can tell me."

"Can you come over?"

"Well, I'm at work, honey. Aren't your grandmother and Uncle Quinn there with you? I know the weather's a little scary, but they will keep you safe."

"They're out looking for Molly. It's just me and Gracie here at Mawmaw's and sometimes the thunder is real loud and the light..."

"Wait." Esther gripped the phone tighter. "Scout, slow down. What do you mean they are out looking for Molly? Is she missing?"

"Yes, ma'am." A sob caught in the child's voice. "Mawmaw made us lay down and take a nap when the power went out and we couldn't watch TV, but Molly was worried about Rambler 'cause he hates thunder."

"How long ago was that, Scout?" Esther stood from the chair and opened her desk drawer, pulling out her purse. "She ran out looking for Rambler and didn't come back?"

"Yes, ma'am. I don't know how long it's been, but Mawmaw and Quinn were fussing at each other. They both left to look for her. Mawmaw came back a while ago and called Daddy 'cause she couldn't find her. I snuck her phone out of her cigarette case before she left. Can you come help us? I don't like it when Mawmaw and Quinn fight."

"I'm on my way, Scout." Esther put the phone to her chest as she passed the reception desk where Darcy Carson sat, staring at her. "I've got to go. Molly Lewis is missing. I'm going out to help hunt for her."

"Go," Darcy said, waving her hand toward the door. "I'll get Blaze to get some people to go help. Be careful in this weather. There are trees down in several places outside of town."

Esther nodded and continued to the exit. "I'll call if they find her." She lifted the phone back to her ear. "Scout?"

"Miss Esther, do you think Molly is dead?"

"No, Scout. Molly is fine." Esther swallowed, keeping her voice steady. "She's probably curled up with Rambler under your house or some place like that. Now you don't go outside. You and Gracie get a pillow and go sit in the hall, okay? Are you at your house or your mawmaw's trailer? I can't remember what you said."

"We're at Mawmaw's. We have a flashlight and are sitting in Mawmaw's bathtub. She said that's the safest place in the house."

"Okay. You hang tight. I'll be right there."

A gust of wind whipped across the almost empty parking lot, blowing Esther's hair around her face. Drake's mother should have already gotten those kids out of that trailer and into his house where it was safer. They weren't under an actual tornado warning, but you didn't wait until that happened to get out of a mobile home. Everybody knew that. She climbed in her car and looked out at the black clouds rolling across the sky. Big fat drops of water began to fall as she pulled out of the lot and headed out of town toward the Lewis place. Trees along the side of the road swayed one way and then the other as she hurried along the country road. Debris littered the pavement, and she swerved a couple of times to miss limbs laying in the road. "Lord, watch over those kids."

Esther pulled into Mrs. Lewis's yard and hurried up the steps of the trailer. Not bothering to knock, she opened the door to the dark living room. Her nostrils flared. Stale cigarette smoke wafted over her. "Scout? Gracie?"

Bumping came from another room, then footsteps running up the hall. "Hey, you two. Let's get you over to your house, okay?"

"Mawmaw said to wait here," Gracie said, her voice full of dread. "She'll be mad if we leave without asking."

"I'll talk to your grandmother. Don't worry." Esther looked around the dark living room, then opened back up the front door. "Scout, leave her phone on the coffee table. Let's go. Y'all run to the car and climb in. We'll get wet, but it'll be okay."

Esther held the door open and let the children run ahead. She shut the door behind them and hurried across the yard, now slippery with black mud mixed with a few blades of grass here and there. She got in the car, her hair and clothing dripping with water, and looked behind her. "When we get to your house, go change clothes and get in the hall, okay?" Both the children nodded as she backed out of the yard and drove the few yards up the road to Drake's house. "Can either of you think of any place Molly might have gone?"

"When Rambler gets scared, he goes down to the pond," Gracie said, staring at Esther's reflection in the rearview mirror. "I told Molly he was probably there, but I didn't know she was going to go find him. I thought she was just going to check on the puppies and come back. I told her Rambler would come back, and she got mad." Gracie's lower lip trembled. "She said I didn't love him anymore since Poochie had puppies, but that's not true."

"It's okay, Gracie." Esther's eyes held Gracie's in the mirror as she pulled to a stop in Drake's yard. "I'll find Molly and Rambler, and everything will be fine." She put the car in park and turned to look at the children. "I'm going to text your grandmother and tell her where you are. If she goes home and looks at her phone, she'll see the message. Can you two go in and do what I said?"

"Yes, ma'am," Scout said, taking Gracie by the hand. "Are you going to find Molly? The path behind the clothesline goes to the pond."

"Yes, Scout. I'm heading that way now. If Quinn or your grandmother get here before I get back, y'all tell them what you told me."

"We tried to." Tears ran down Gracie's cheeks. "They were yelling at each other and wouldn't listen to us."

Esther leaned across the backseat and kissed the girl on the head. "Go with your brother. I'll be back soon, okay?"

"Okay." Gracie sniffed and slid across the seat behind Scout. The children climbed out of the backseat and ran through the rain and mud into their house.

Esther watched the door close behind them, then climbed out of the car. Where were Quinn and his mother? Drake should have never left his kids. She hurried around the house, the wind at her back pushing her along. "Lord, help me find that baby. I love her like she's my own. Please let me find her."

Chapter Eighteen

Drake leaned forward, staring at the taillights in front of him, barely visible through the wind and the rain. It was five in the evening, but with the clouds and the storm, it looked more like eight at night. The pilot delayed the helicopter to fly him in from the oil rig until the wind and rain died down, but he'd finally gotten inland. That was about it, though. The further he drove toward home, the heavier the rain fell, and the slower the traffic became. He had been on the road an hour and a half, and there was still a long way to go.

He rubbed his hands against his eyes and leaned forward, staring through the rain pounding the windshield. Nobody was answering his calls. That couldn't be good. Quinn had texted one time since he'd gotten in his truck.

> Momma thinks she might have tried walking into town. She's going up the road one way, and I'm going the other direction. Already checked everywhere in the yard.

Why did Momma think she would try to walk to town?

She's going to see Esther. That's got to be it. They had seen her at church the Sunday he was in from work. Molly had run to Esther and wrapped her arms around the poor woman's legs, begging her to sit with them. Esther, being Esther, had patiently explained why she needed to sit with her grandmother instead. Molly, being Molly, had insisted on sitting with Esther and Esther's grandparents. The service was starting, and Drake started pulling the child away quietly. Esther had stopped him and let the child sit with her, assuring him it was fine. After church, on the drive home, the kids had talked about Esther and how much they missed her. So much for all of them getting over her.

"Dad, can't you get Miss Esther to come see us again?" Gracie had asked. "We love Miss Esther."

"I know kids, but Miss Esther is a busy lady. We can't expect her to spend all her days with us."

"She used to." Molly's lower lip had poked out, and she'd looked accusingly at Drake. "Why can't she now?"

"Because Daddy made her cry." Scout turned from staring out the window of the truck. "I heard one of the lunch ladies talking about it at school. They said Miss Esther had to see a head doctor because of Daddy."

"What's a head doctor? Is Miss Esther sick?" Gracie asked, her brow pulled low. "Daddy, why did you make Miss Esther cry?"

"Scout, you shouldn't listen to other people's conversations." Drake had wanted to smack a couple of cafeteria workers in the back of the head at that moment. "Miss Esther is not sick. We just had a little disagreement." He had pulled into the grocery store parking lot and unbuckled his seat belt. "Come on. Let's go get ice cream. I have to leave tonight. I want you to make me a banana split like you did last time."

The illusion that pushing Esther out of their lives had not

affected his kids had busted that Sunday, but had Molly really run away this morning to find her? He picked his phone up from the seat beside him and thumbed down to Esther's number. He kept his eyes on the taillights in front of him as her phone rang, then went to voice mail. "Esther, I'm on my way home. Molly's missing, and we think she may be walking in to town to come see you. Please call me. I..." The last word hung in the air. He pressed the disconnect button and tossed the phone back on the seat. He stared through the windshield, no longer hearing the steady rhythm of the wipers mixing with the background of falling rain. He couldn't tell her that he was scared. Scared of loving her, scared of losing her like he lost Paige. That he had taken the coward's way out and ran back to his loneliness because he couldn't stand the idea of opening his heart up to her, then trying to go on without her.

The rain started to slow, and the car ahead of him picked up a little speed. He needed coffee. Coffee and a second to try to call Quinn. If he couldn't get in touch with Quinn, then he would call the Carson's Bayou police. At this rate, the sun would be setting by the time he got home. Every person he knew needed to be out looking for his baby. Every person would be able to do that... except him.

"Molly!" Esther cupped her hands around her mouth and yelled again. The grass, tall and wet, slapped against her thin scrubs, but she pushed forward through the woods away from Drake's back yard. The wind and rain were slowing, and she picked up her pace. *Lord, keep the snakes under the rocks and out of this tall grass near me.*

She stopped and turned her head to the side. A faint sound came from up ahead. A barking dog... Rambler. "Molly." She ran, ignoring the sticky black mud splattering up on her legs as her tennis shoes trudged through the puddles and saturated ground. "I'm coming, Molly."

Esther stopped at the edge of the pond, her heart jumping into her throat. "Molly — don't move. I'm coming in to get you."

Molly stared up from the water at Esther, her face a mask of fear. Her arms were clutched around a branch of an old tree, blown over into the water in the distant past, slimy with green moss. Rambler, who had been standing on the tree trunk above where Molly was hanging on, nimbly trotted across the slippery surface of the dead tree and back to the water's edge. He whined at Esther and ran back to the edge of the water, urging her to follow.

Esther treaded behind the dog, wading through the sticky mud to where the tree had been uprooted. She climbed over the exposed roots, raised from the base of the tree like spider legs sticking out in all directions, and stepped onto the tree trunk, leaving the dog behind her. She had never been known for her athletic prowess, but her fear for the child's safety gave her strength to step out onto the slippery surface of the trunk as it shifted under her weight.

"Molly." Esther kneeled down and got on all fours. "It sure was brave of you to come out here and rescue Rambler." The child stared at Esther, her huge eyes following Esther's slow progression toward her. How long had she been there? It was summer, and even though the storm had dropped the sweltering summer temps some, it was still warm. That didn't matter. If the exhausted child had been drenched in the cold rain, then fell in the tepid pond, she could be going into shock. There was no telling how many times she had been under before grabbing the tree limb, or how much of the nasty pond she had swallowed and gotten into her lungs.

Esther crept along the log on her hands and knees at the pace of a turtle, talking to the child the entire time. After an eternity, she lay down on her belly and extended her arm. "Molly." She reached down with one hand and grabbed a fistful of the child's pink unicorn shirt, soaked and stained with slime and mud. She hung onto the tree trunk for dear life with the other. "Honey, I need you to grab my arm, okay?"

The little hand closest to Esther let go of the limb and grabbed Esther's arm in a vice-like grip. "Good job, big girl. Now, I'm going to pull you up when I count to three. You kick your legs and push toward me. Got it?"

Molly's head nodded. Esther let her legs separate, slipping into the water on either side of the log to help her keep her balance. She had no idea how deep or snaky this pond was, but she didn't intend to find out either.

Alligators infested a lot of lakes and ponds around the area. "One." Of course, this pond didn't necessarily have alligators in it. "Two." Even so, they needed to get this done. "Three." Esther pressed her chest against the cool, wet moss covering the log and pulled the child toward her with everything she had. Molly slid forward, climbing onto the log, then onto Esther's back, attaching herself to Esther like a leech. "Wrap your arms around my neck," Esther said. She coughed as Molly's arms lunged out around her. "Not too tight, okay? I need to breathe." The grip lessened a fraction. "That's better."

Molly's little body lay cool against Esther's back like an ice pack. How long had she been in the water? "Okay. Let's crawfish off this thing and get back to the house and get us something warm to drink." Somewhere off in the distance, a siren blared. "You hear that?" Esther continued to scoot backwards against the grain of everything growing on the log.

Rough surfaces cut into her skin as her scrub shirt rolled up under her. A splash caught her attention, and she looked into the water as her cell phone floated out of sight into the murk. "I bet that's somebody coming to look for you."

They made their way back to the base of the trunk and Esther pushed herself into a sitting position, Molly still on her back. She swung her legs around and scooted on her bottom the last couple of feet toward the bank.

"Molly, I need to stand up. Can you climb across the roots ahead of me onto the ground?" The child, the fearless dare devil, didn't move or make a sound. "It's okay." Esther reached back and took hold of one of Molly's legs, still holding onto the log with her other hand. She pulled the girl's leg forward around her waist on one side, then switched hands and did the same thing on the other. "You hang on, and I'll piggy-back you over the roots."

Esther stretched her feet downward in the water but did not find the bottom of the pond. She couldn't try climbing up the slick bank from the deep water with Molly on her back. She wasn't strong enough and would drown them both. She leaned on her side toward the spidery leg roots reaching up like sharp little tentacles and hoisted herself over the spiny appendages, closing her eyes as they pricked and pierced her skin. She clawed her way over the base of the trunk onto the oozy bank.

"We did it, Molly," Esther said, pushing up on all fours when she reached the soggy but solid ground. Rambler, who had been pacing back and forth on the bank for the entire time, came over, wiggling from one end to the other like a young puppy, and began licking Molly in the face. Esther gently released Molly's little hands from around her neck and stood her in front of her. She raised up, then reached down, and picked up the petrified child.

"Look." Molly's teeth chattered with the single word.

Esther breathed out a sigh of relief. The poor thing was usually a chatterbox. Her silence was not a good sign. She looked to where the child was pointing. Sunshine peaked through from behind a patch of gray clouds, and above that a rainbow painted the sky. "I think the storm is over."

Molly didn't answer, but let out a deep rumbling cough. Esther started back through the grass toward the house with Molly on her hip. They were out of the pond, but not out of the woods. She needed to get Molly warm and dry. The child was prone to respiratory infections. Pneumonia was probably already developing. If she had her phone, she would call Barlow and tell him what was going on and to send an ambulance. That couldn't happen with her phone at the bottom of the pond. The soaked, cold child coughed again, and her shivers vibrated against Esther's wet scrub shirt. "Hang on Molly. We're going to go for a run."

Voices up ahead through the trees called Molly's name. Esther stopped. "Out here," she yelled. "Hurry." She took off running again, her side hurting something awful, but that pain would have to wait.

Several men appeared through the woods, and Quinn ran toward them, leading the way. He took Molly from Esther's arms and snuggled her close to his chest. "You gave me quite a scare little one," he whispered, tears in his voice.

"We need to get her to the ER." Esther hurried, trying to keep up with Quinn's long legs as they made their way back up the path. "I'm afraid she might have pneumonia."

"We need to get you checked out, too."

"Me?" Esther frowned, looking at Quinn's grim expression. She looked down at the red stains on her scrub top. "Oh. I'm bleeding."

Chapter Nineteen

"Her chest x-ray shows some patches in her lower lobes, but she's responding well to the breathing treatments." Barlow patted Drake on the shoulder. "She's going to be okay, man."

"I don't know how I'm ever going to thank everyone." Drake ran his hand through his hair, his eyes searching the ER cubical for the answer to his question. "I should have got in touch with the sheriff as soon as Quinn and Momma called me, but I didn't think she was really missing. I just figured she was in one of her usual hiding places." His mouth turned down, his shoulders slumped forward, mirroring the weight of his regret and guilt for everyone to see. "If Darcy and Blaze hadn't gotten the church folks out to help find her, she could have..."

"That's what families do," Barlow said, guiding Drake over to a nearby chair. "But I need to tell you, friend. The person you should be talking to is my sister. She's the one who saved Molly's life. I think you know that."

"Yeah." Drake sat down on the cold metal chair and

looked at the man he had known since childhood. "I just don't know how to face her, Bar. I did her so wrong."

"Yeah, you did." Barlow sat in the seat beside Drake. "I have to tell you that you were not on my good side for quite a while. If it wouldn't have upset Esther even more, I probably would have come over and, well... actually let you whip my tail, if I'm honest." He grinned and shoved Drake in the shoulder like he did when they were kids. "I'd have gotten a few licks in though." His face sobered. "Why did you do her like that, Drake? You really hurt her. You knew how she felt about you, right? You had to. Everybody else did."

"I didn't...at least not at first." Drake flopped backwards against the chair and stretched his long legs in front of him. "I mean, I thought she liked me, and I liked her. It was all happening so fast, though."

"Not for her." Barlow stood up and walked over to the little coffeepot sitting on the counter. He poured two Styrofoam cups full of the black liquid that someone had brewed in the last twenty-four hours. "You shouldn't have led her on if you weren't feeling the same way. I mean." He stepped over and handed Drake one of the cups. "You might not have felt as strongly as she did, but if you were only a friend, why were you dating her and snooping around my house?"

"I wasn't." Drake took a sip of the coffee, and his nostrils flared. He set his cup down on the floor at his feet. "I mean, I wanted what she... I want more than friendship. I still do, but she wanted." Drake stopped, still unable to put his fears into words.

"Look." Barlow swallowed a gulp of coffee. "I'm not the one you need to be talking to, and you know it. My sister has risked life and limb today for your kids, and you haven't even been in to see her." He stood up and stared down at Drake. "You need to man up and be the Drake Lewis I know. I don't understand what's going on with you, but you've never shied away from anything you wanted." Barlow's eyes narrowed. "Is that it? Are you not going in to see her because you know how she feels, and you don't want to be bothered?"

"No." Drake stood up. "I'm not like that, Barlow." He looked up at the ceiling, staring at the white tiles with the little black holes. Barlow was right. He could either take the risk and move forward with Esther—or get out of her life for good. It was not fair to her... or his kids to go back and forth like he was doing, seeing her on Sundays at church, searching for her during the week. "I love your sister." The words came out in a whisper, almost like a declaration of defeat. "I love her." He turned and looked at Barlow. "I don't think I can handle loving her and losing her."

Barlow's eyebrows raised. "Paige?" He looked at Drake, his whole body oozing with defeat. "Man, you got to let go of the fear. Give all that to God. What if Esther hadn't cared enough today to do what she did? You could have lost your child." He put his hand on Drake's shoulder and squeezed. "What happened with Paige was terrible, but Esther is not Paige. She's tough as nails and healthy as a horse. Even without that, she's alive until God decides to take her home, same as the rest of us. When we die is God's business, brother. You've got to..."

Code Blue, second floor. Code Blue, second floor. Barlow pulled his hand back as the announcement blared out again. "Got to run, Drake. Go talk to Esther... but maybe talk to God first."

ESTHER LIFTED her hospital gown and ran her fingers across the clean white bandage secured to her right side with wide paper tape. The entire front of her abdomen looked like she had been in a cat fight and lost, but only one of the cuts required stitches. It wasn't too bad either, just four closed the gash up nicely. The tetanus shot in her arm and the Rocephin shot in her hip were way more painful than any of the care to her middle.

She adjusted the pile of blankets around her legs and moved her hips on the padded exam table, trying to find a more comfortable spot. As soon as her grandparents arrived with fresh clothes from her house, she would get out of here. She hadn't wanted to bother them and would have put back on her slimy scrubs, but Barlow said those had been red bagged as hazardous waste already. There was no telling what her grandmother would pull from the closet to bring her to wear. Since her phone was at the bottom of Drake's pond, she couldn't make a call and tell her that sweats and t-shirts were in the bottom of the chest of drawers.

She leaned her head back and closed her eyes. The steady line of people coming in to check on her had finally slowed. She had ridden with Molly in the ambulance to the hospital as soon as they got out of the woods. Quinn, the kids, and Drake's mother had followed in Quinn's truck.

Molly did not let Esther leave her side, finding her voice, and effectively caterwauling until everyone did her bidding. Someone had pressed a wad of gauze into Esther's hands when she refused to leave the child to be cared for herself. The emergency room team assessed and x-rayed Molly. Esther had looked on, applying pressure to her side, stopping the oozing trickle of blood from her gash. Shortly after that, Drake's mother came in, and a nurse rolled Esther's wheelchair out to her own exam room while Molly was distracted. Barlow gave Esther frequent updates on Molly's condition. They were moving the child upstairs to a room, but every indication pointed to a release in a couple of days with a full recovery.

"Can I give you a hug?" Quinn came in with Scout and

Gracie a little while later. "The last time I tried seems like I recall you punching me in the gut or something."

"That was fifteen years ago." Esther grinned at Drake's handsome little brother. "Yes, all hugs are welcome today." She visited with Quinn and the kids for about twenty minutes, listening to them tell and retell the events of the day as their brains tried to process everything that happened.

"Quinn said since Rambler helped you find Molly that he can sleep with me tonight," Gracie said, laying her head over on Esther's arm. "We have to give him a bath first, though. He's all dirty, and Daddy won't like it if he gets mud in my bed."

"That's probably a good idea." Esther stroked Gracie's hair and looked at the foot of her makeshift bed where Quinn stood. "Is Drake here?"

"He should be pulling in within the hour. I'm sure he will come see you after he checks on Molly."

That was over three hours ago. Drake's mother had come in and apologized for her harsh attitude toward Esther over the years. Esther had assured her all was well, especially since she hadn't known the bad feelings existed. Darcy, Blaze, and nearly everyone from her Sunday school class had poured in, along with several others from the church who had started searching for the child as soon as Darcy had sent out the call... but no Drake.

"Esther?"

Esther opened her eyes and looked at the man standing in front of the curtain enclosure. "I thought you decided you didn't want to see me."

"I." Drake stepped forward and stuck out his hand. "I needed to get myself together after I saw Molly. I went by the gift shop and got you this. Once Molly's home, we'll all take you out to eat to show you how grateful we are for what you've done."

Esther's fingers brushed against Drake's as she took the white rosebud from his hand. That old familiar ache pulled at her heart, full force, like it did before the therapy, before her new resolve to move on. "Thank you." She looked down at the flower, blinking away the tears. *I can't go back to this. It hurts too much. I won't survive.* She raised her head and pulled in her lips, biting down, pulling up courage. "I don't think. No. I know I can't handle seeing you and the kids again the way we were before."

"Esther, I..."

"Let me finish." Esther swallowed, trying to push away the tears, but they squeezed out and ran down her cheeks. "You about broke me, Drake. I can't let that happen again. I love... your kids." She looked away from his eyes, piercing into hers, and swiped her hand across her cheek. "I can't do this halfway anymore. I tried, but I just can't. Let this be your thank you. I did what I did because I love your family." She shrugged and looked back at his slumped shoulders. "Today I am absolutely positive that I couldn't love any children I gave birth to a bit more than I love Molly and Gracie and Scout. But it is wrong for me to flitter in and out of their lives the way I've been doing."

She sniffed and looked around for a tissue. Drake stepped closer and pulled a brown paper towel from the dispenser on the wall. He handed it to her. "I want more than being a friend, she said. "You don't. It's time we part ways for good."

"Esther..."

Esther lifted her hand. "Let me say what I need to say. I'm going to start attending a different church. I will talk to the pastor and explain why. That way, the kids won't see me when you are in from work, and they can move on, too. All I need you to do is make sure when you bring them into the clinic that you tell Darcy to let me know. I'll stay out of sight until you are gone."

"Esther, I want more than friendship."

Esther pulled in a shuddering breath. "You say that today, Drake, but what about tomorrow when all of this is over? No." She shook her head as he reached out. "I don't trust you. I'm sorry."

"Esther, please."

"Drake." Tears rolled freely down her cheeks. *Push on.* "I can't."

Esther watched Drake's face, his eyes begging her to listen, then resigning in defeat. He turned and made his way out of the exam room, his steps slow, silent. *I had to. He doesn't know what he wants, and I can't go through that again. This is the right thing. It hurts now, but it will get better. It did before. It will again.*

She sat up on the exam table and pushed the call light. She needed to go home, with or without new clothes. The hospital gown would have to do. It was time to get her life back to normal. Her old life, the one before she got a taste of what it could have been. The gash on her side throbbed as she slid her feet to the floor. She would heal. Some wounds took a while, like the one in her heart, but she was strong. *I know that now. I just have to endure.*

Chapter Twenty

D rake sat at Molly's bedside, leaning forward, his chin resting in the palm of his hand, listening to the child's steady chatter. The nebulizer treatment they gave her a while back had keyed her up. and she was talking a blue streak.

"Rambler was out on that log and couldn't come back. He was so scared, Daddy." Molly paused and released a deep, loose sounding cough. "The lightning and thunder was so scary, but I couldn't let him fall in the pond and drown, Daddy. I thought he couldn't swim, like me."

"I know you thought you were doing the right thing, Molly, but you might have drowned yourself."

"I didn't though. I walked out there on that log and almost had him calmed down, but a big pop of thunder made him jump again."

An iron grip of fear squeezed in Drake's chest as he listened to his daughter tell all about the incident. *Thank you, God, for protecting my girl.* "Is that when you fell into the pond?"

"We both did, me and Rambler. But he swam over to the

edge and climbed out." Molly's lips pushed into a firm line. "Dumb old dog. He climbed right out of the pond, Daddy, and left me in it. I wouldn't ever do that to anybody, would you?"

"Well, Rambler is just a dog." Drake raked a butter colored curl out of Molly's eyes. "I hope you understand how dangerous a situation you put yourself in. What if Miss Esther hadn't come along and gotten you out?"

"I was scared, but I knew she was coming." Molly turned her round eyes up to her father. "Since you were gone away, I prayed and told God to send Miss Esther or Quinn to come get me. I knew Mawmaw couldn't do it. She's too old."

Drake sat up straight in his chair as his daughter coughed. She finally caught her breath and continued to rattle on about how scared she had been when the rain kept hitting her in the face and splattering into the pond, making it hard to breathe. She described how she went under several times because the limbs were slimy, and she kept losing her grip. He stroked her hair, letting her share the excitement of the day to clear her mind and the rush of the medication to help fight the congestion work through her little body. She finally dozed, her chest rising and falling gently, interrupted every few minutes by a deep reverberating cough. He picked up his Coke sitting on the bedside table and took a long drink. A call for a doctor sounded over the loudspeaker in the hallway, but Molly slept on, exhausted.

There was one positive thing to take away from all of this. He couldn't go back offshore. He was their father. Nobody would ever fill those shoes but him. *How do I make ends meet and still be home every night with the kids?* He set the bottle back down and stared at his daughter. *Thank you, God, for letting her stay here with us. For watching over her even when I wasn't doing my part.*

He rubbed his hands across his eyes and raked his fingers

down his face. There was also the mistake, the one he'd been ignoring. It was time to deal with that one, too. *I love Esther. Why was I so hardheaded about this before? Because I was scared of losing her.* Not now.

After today, it was plainly obvious that God was in control of when and where everyone would leave this earth. Why did it take something like this, like almost losing his little one, to make him see that he couldn't worry about when or how a person would die? He had to live today and leave tomorrow to God. He'd heard that in sermons before, but some stuff didn't really stick, at least not for him, until the reality of it slapped him in the face.

She didn't want him. She wanted them to go their separate ways. What did he expect? To waltz in the hospital and sweep her off her feet? *Idiot.* He took out his phone and pulled up the picture he snapped at the park that day of Esther and the kids eating snow cones. *I'm gonna win her back —show her she can trust me, depend on me. I have to. She still loves me. She has to.*

But how? He had really hurt her. He slipped his phone in his pocket and leaned his head against the back of the chair, closing his eyes. *I can't force this. I have to take my time, show her that I'm not going anywhere, no matter what.* His head lulled to the side, his eyes drooping closed as his legs stretched out under the edge of the hospital bed, his arms crossed over his chest. He loved her. He would win her back, be the man she needed.

The summer sun beat down on Esther in full force as she walked up the sidewalk to her front porch from the mailbox.

Another day, another letter. It had been four weeks since that day at the pond. The day in the hospital when she told Drake that she didn't want anything to do with him. Since then, she had talked to her pastor, explaining why she was changing churches. He had advised against it.

"You can't run from this, Esther," the pastor said after hearing what transpired between the two at the hospital. "Talk it out with Drake first. Listen to what he has to say. If you feel that you need to distance yourself from the Lewis family, then go ahead. You need to see where he stands on all this before you just upturn your life like this. That's not fair to you."

Of course, she didn't listen to him, or her counselor... or Barlow... or Granny. She didn't go to church at all that first Sunday. Molly had come home from the hospital that day. She had called and gotten an update on her status from the pediatrician every afternoon during the child's time there.

At their church too many people would be asking too many questions. People would assume she would fill them in on how the child was doing. That would lead to questions about her and Drake. People would take sides, defend her, and put down on Drake. That was not what she wanted or needed. She wasn't ready to face all of that. The last thing she wanted was to make a spectacle of herself by squalling in the church parking lot.

The next week, she attended the enormous church on the corner near the Presbyterian church. She slipped in the back right at the start time, then slipped out before the invitation, effectively avoiding actually talking to a single person. That worked like a charm until last Sunday. She had stepped out of the pew and into the foyer to leave as she had the other two Sundays, but this time a man, a tall, attractive man, followed.

Langston Wade introduced himself and invited her to Sunday school and to join their fellowship group that met on

Sunday evenings. She thanked him and managed to still get away before the service was over. Now, however, she was sure other people from the church would start seeking her out in an effort to make her feel welcome. All those conversations would lead back to Molly... and Drake. *I have to face this. I'm running from the inevitable.*

A few days later, Esther looked down at the now familiar light blue envelope in her hand. Drake's handwriting scrawled his address across the top and hers across the bottom. She stuck the letter under the water bill and climbed the porch steps. Inside her house, she laid the water bill on the bar and continued upstairs. She slid open the top drawer of her dresser and pulled out the stack of blue envelopes, twenty-nine to be exact, all in Drake's handwriting, all unopened.

She plopped down on her bed and crossed her legs, fanning the envelopes out in front of her. He texted once a week, on Sunday afternoons like clockwork, asking if she would talk to him. She could block him. She should, since she didn't want to see him... but...

"You need to talk to the guy." Barlow poked his head in her bedroom door, his lips turned down in a frown. "I know in the beginning I said to stay away from him."

"That's right, you did."

"Just listen." Barlow stepped into the bedroom and looked down at the envelopes. "You scared the daylights out of the man before, sis. He had cold feet, and I admit, messed everything up. You didn't help matters by coming on so strong, either."

"Well, why don't you tell me what you really think?" Sarcasm oozed from Esther's words as she stared up at her twin. "You don't know what that man put me through."

"You're right. I don't exactly. I did see you not eating, hear you crying, and watch you turn into a zombie while you were working all this out. So, yeah, I have an idea of what you went through." Barlow eased down on the bed beside Esther. "But I can tell you one thing, you are putting him through the same thing right now—maybe even worse. Have you seen him at all since the day at the hospital?"

"No." Esther reached down and touched the edge of the latest letter. "Well, not up close. I've seen him driving by the clinic a few times, and at the park, but so far I've always figured out a way to avoid him."

"Esther." Barlow leaned his shoulder against his sister. "Are you happy doing this? Is this what you want?"

"No." Esther swallowed and laid her head over on Barlow's shoulder. "Of course not. I'm miserable, but what if he rejects me again, Bar? It hurt so bad."

"I know." Barlow squeezed Esther's shoulders. "I'm praying you two work all this out. I've talked to Drake and..."

"What?" Esther's head shot up and her eyes bored into Barlow's. "When. What about?"

"That day at the hospital and then a few times at church." Barlow matched Esther's stare. "You forget, I didn't change churches. I still see him on Sundays when I'm not working."

"What did he say?"

"Oh, no." Barlow stood up. "If you want to know what he's thinking, you need to talk to him yourself, or." He pointed to the envelopes piled on the bed. "Or at least read his letters. You're being kind of childish."

Esther's lips poked out. She watched Barlow leave her room, then gathered up the envelopes. Her forehead wrinkled, thinking about everything Barlow said. Why did he insist on getting in her business? "I'm not being childish. I'm being careful." After a few minutes, she stood from the bed and listened to a knocking on the front door. "That's odd," she mumbled, dropping the envelopes back in the drawer. "Why don't they ring the bell?"

Esther stepped into the hall. The splatter of the shower

from Barlow's bathroom came from his end of the house. *Bump, bump.* Yes, that was definitely the front door. She hurried down the steps, into the foyer, and jerked open the door. "Can I..."

Drake's truck pulled away from the curb in front of her house. "What in the world?" She stepped out onto the porch to look around. After his little tree climbing stunt from before, who knew what he was up to this time? She looked up and down the porch for any signs that he'd been there. Nothing looked out of the ordinary. She turned to go back inside. A letter, written on paper the same shade of blue as all the others, hung on the front door, tacked into the wood. PLEASE READ ME was written in big, bold letters on the first page.

Esther looked over her shoulder, making sure no one was watching, then ripped the papers down, leaving the tack stuck in place. She ran upstairs to her room and shut her door behind her. She flopped onto her bed, ignoring the squeaking bedsprings as she slowly lifted the first page and began reading.

> Dear Esther,
>
> I heard from an inside source that so far you have not opened any of my letters. I vowed to be patient in my desire to prove to you that I am serious in my feelings for you, but patience is proving to be harder for me than I imagined. I have to say that other than my drive home from the oil rig on the day you rescued Molly, this month has been the longest, hardest wait I have endured since Paige's death.

It's not that I just want to see you, to talk to you. I need to talk to you. I need to see you, to hear your voice, to know what you are thinking about, to be near you.

I have no right to ask you for anything after the way I treated you, but Esther... have mercy. Please let me explain. If you don't want to have anything to do with me after hearing me out, I promise I will somehow leave you alone forever. It will break my heart, but if that is what you want...

Love,

Drake

Chapter Twenty-One

Drake tugged on his tie and looked around. People were giving him odd glances before cutting their eyes away, some were even laughing. *Yes. I'm over-dressed for the snow cone stand. I know it, people.*

This was not the place he had in mind when he envisioned his meeting with Esther. He figured he would show up at her door with flowers, maybe even candy, and take her to a fancy romantic restaurant. But desperate times called for desperate measures. When she texted him yesterday afternoon after he nailed the letter to her door, he would have met in the Carson's Bayou swamps outside of town if she had asked him to.

The suit had seemed like a good idea in his air-conditioned bedroom, trying to figure out how to impress the woman he loved at a snow cone stand. Now, with perspiration pouring from his forehead, sweat trickling down his spine, the idea held less merit.

"You look nice."

Drake turned to the voice and shifted his weight from one

foot to the other. She was even more beautiful than he had dreamed about for the last month. "I look ridiculous."

"Maybe just a little." Esther's eyes creased at the corners. "Are you going somewhere afterwards? You're a little over-dressed for the snow cone stand."

"No." Drake grinned as a drop of sweat dripped off the tip of his nose. "Only here. There's this woman that I'm trying to impress, so I'm putting my best foot forward."

Esther pushed her fingers to her lips, covering her smile. "Must be some woman. It's supposed to get up to one hundred degrees today." She glanced down at her tank top and blue jean shorts. "Do you think this woman is impressed with clothes?"

"No." Drake reached up and loosened his tie. "She's the type of woman that is impressed by character, actions, what a person stands for, what they believe. Unfortunately for me, my actions lately have been sorely lacking and not lining up with what I know in my heart is right." He slipped the knot from the tie and pulled it from his neck. "So, I'm having to do everything... pull out all the stops to make her see that I'm sorry." Drake watched Esther's smile fade as her eyes turn somber. "Can we talk? He asked, his voice suddenly soft. "Please?"

"Yes." She nodded, not offering any other words.

Drake slipped off the suit coat and looked at his long-sleeved white shirt, already damp with perspiration. "Do you mind holding onto this while I get us a couple of snow cones? I am literally melting."

"I'll wait for you over at the bench near the duck pond."

Drake watched Esther stroll away, his suit coat draped over her arm. He turned and stepped up to the snow cone stand in the little moveable trailer. The owner relocated the business from place to place throughout the warm months of the year. He often parked across from the school from March through May to get the after-school customers and near the high school football stadium for the junior high games in September before the weather got chilly. During the summer when school was out, he could be found in the parking lot at the edge of the park.

Drake ordered a pickle juice snow cone for him and a strawberry cheesecake one for Esther. He hurried over to the bench near the walking trail and pulled his lips together in a thin line. He set the snow cones on the bench and pulled the tail of his dress shirt from his pants. Several people stared, not even pretending to look away. He unbuttoned his sweaty shirt and peeled it away from his equally sweaty undershirt. *The show stops here, folks. I'm not streaking, just trying to keep from suffocating.*

He tossed the damp dress shirt over his arm and picked up the Styrofoam cups. A warm breeze caressed his neck and arms and he smiled. *Putting on that suit was just plain ole stupid.* He strode across the lawn to the duck pond at the bottom of the grassy play area. "Take your pick." Drake held both cups out, and Esther looked up from the bench at the pale green and deep red mounds of ice in the cups.

"Your face is still red," she said, reaching for the sweet snow cone. "I was concerned that you were headed toward a heat stroke."

"Me too." Drake scooped up a mound of the sour flavored ice and put in his mouth. "Can I sit with you?"

"Yes."

"Esther." Drake looked down at the cup in his hands, then lifted his head, watching the ducks float across the nearby water. The aroma of wisteria drifted through the air from the trees on the backside of the pond. "I wish I could take back that day at the Gumbo Hut."

"I don't."

Drake turned and stared at Esther, his brow furrowed. "I was a jerk. I didn't mean to be a jerk, honestly, I didn't—but I was a class A jerk. I hurt you, and I need you to forgive me."

"I have forgiven you, Drake. I thought I forgave you before... when I started seeing a counselor, but I hadn't. I wanted you to suffer, like I had suffered." She looked down at her hands, then slowly lifted her eyes back to his face. "I finally forgave you yesterday, after I took your letter off my door. I have to be honest. As hard and as painful as all this has been, I'm glad it happened, not what happened with Molly, of course, but the *thing*... at the Gumbo Hut."

"I don't understand." Drake stared at Esther, her shoulders relaxed, leaning back against the park bench. "How could you be glad that I was, well, mean to you? Which I plan on explaining to you in a second."

"Drake." Esther's lips turned up in a soft smile. "I had put you on a pedestal so big and tall that there was no way on this earth that you wouldn't eventually tumble off of it." She reached up and tucked a wayward curl behind her ear. "You had become my all in all, that place should only be filled by One, and unlike you, that One really can walk on water." She picked up her little plastic spoon and stirred her cup of ice. "Since that day, I have done a lot of soul searching and realized that I can't let any man take the place in my heart that only belongs to God. That's wrong. I was wrong."

"But Esther..."

"Let me say this, then I promise that you can tell me whatever you want to say." Esther lifted the red ice to her lips and waited. Drake nodded for her to continue. "Then yesterday, after reading your letter, I realized that I was enjoying keeping you away, hoping I was hurting you the way you hurt me." Her lips pulled into a flat line, and her eyes wandered around the park, filling with tears. "I'm sorry for that. I don't consider myself vindictive, but..."

"Esther." Drake reached out and touched his fingertips to the top of her hand, his voice low. "The reason I said I didn't want to have children with you was because I was scared." His hand covered hers, a different heat creeping across his chest. "I was terrified of bringing you into my life, then losing you the way I lost Paige."

"But Drake..."

Drake reached up and touched his finger to her red stained lips. "I was wrong. Having you in my life is a gift from God. I can't control the amount of time we have here together. What happened with Molly drove that home to me like a sword through the heart." He ran his finger along her bottom lip, scooting closer to her as he spoke. "All I can do is ask you—beg you to give me another chance. If you want us to have ten more kids, we can. I don't care. As long as you will take me back." Esther's hand reached up and touched Drake's lips. A wave of longing washed over him more intense than he had ever felt before. "I know that my life is not right unless you're in it."

Esther leaned forward and brushed her lips against Drake's. She sat back, her eyes wide. "Um. I uh."

Drake's hand reached through Esther's thick caramel curls and drew her mouth back to his, kissing her the way he had been wanting to do for weeks. Freezing cold suddenly flooded his lap, pulling his mind back from where he wanted so desperately to go. He jerked away from Esther, her eyes closed, her lips slightly parted. His huge eyes looked down at the pile of green ice. "Looks like this suit is going to the cleaners," he said, staring at the pickle juice snow cone spilled on his legs.

"Here." Esther coughed, clearing her throat, then scooped

up a spoonful of her strawberry cheesecake ice and raised it to his lips. "I'll share mine with you. It's better anyway."

Drake opened his mouth and let Esther slip the spoon between his lips. "Does this mean you'll take me back?"

"I'll take you back, Drake Lewis, but the truth is, I never really let you go. I just had to figure out where you belonged."

Epilogue

"Mom!" Fourteen-year-old Molly bounced down the staircase of the Lewis home at her usual breakneck speed. "I can't find my cheer uniform. Tonight's Scout's last game. I have to get there on time, and I have to look right." She stopped at the bottom of the stairs and plopped her hand on her hip. "Mom?"

"I hear you." Esther lifted her head from where she was looking over Dane's alphabet letters. The boy's eyes narrowed as he stared at his big sister, mirroring her expression to a tea. "It's hanging in the laundry room," Esther said. "I took it out of the dryer last night so it wouldn't wrinkle... like I told you to do if you remember."

"You're the best." Molly hurried by the bar, kissing Esther on the cheek as she passed. "Is Gracie coming straight from the library to the game? She better not be late. You probably need to call her, Mom."

Esther rolled her eyes. Molly was born to boss. Over the years, time and love had curbed her strong will from a know-it-all child to a confident teen, but she still loved to voice her opinion whenever it popped into her head.

"Scout is picking up Gracie and then dropping by to get you." She glanced over at the clock on the microwave. "If anyone is going to make y'all late, it appears to be you."

"Not a chance." Molly stepped out of the laundry room, zipping up her cheer skirt. "I've got to fix my hair, and I'm good to go. Don't worry about me."

Esther watched her youngest daughter disappear back up the stairs of her family home, the home they had moved into shortly after she and Drake married. They dated for two years. Drake refused to marry until he finished his welding course at the college and was able to secure a solid job in the next parish.

"I want us to start on a firm foundation," Drake said, when the kids asked him when Esther would be their real momma. "I graduate in six months. We will marry and be a true family after that."

The wedding had taken place in the park, near the duck pond, a simple affair with Quinn being the best man. Esther's parents had come to town for the ceremony, and Drake's mother and brother, Hank, along with the kids and her grandparents, had rounded out the group.

Darcy Carson had helped Drake plan a surprise reception at the church for the couple. The memory still warmed Esther's heart. Barlow's present had been the biggest surprise of all. "I've got a new job, Sis. I'm moving to Alabama. The house is yours."

"Momma."

"Hmmm?" Esther blinked away the memories and looked at her youngest son. "Did you say something?"

"I said Daddy's truck drove up. Are we finished? I want to hide behind the couch and scare him when he comes in."

"Be my guest." Esther tussled Dane's curly brown hair, watching him slide from the bar stool and hurry toward the living room where Drake always came in, laying his keys on the coffee table.

"Esther?" Drake's voice filled the house. "You got my clothes ready? I've got to hurry so we won't be late..."

Squealing, giggles, and growls cut Drake's sentence short. Dane raced to the kitchen, followed by Drake, close on his heels. Esther watched Drake grab their youngest son, tickling him, then tossing the boy over his shoulder and heading upstairs to clean up for the big football game. A horn tooted from the front yard, and Molly hurried down the stairs, kissing her daddy and little brother as she passed.

"Mom, make sure you and Dad do the wave when we do the cheer. Tell Dane to get on Daddy's shoulders so he can catch some candy when I throw it in the stands." Molly threw a kiss in Esther's direction, then disappeared. The door slammed a couple of seconds later, rattling their family picture hanging in the foyer.

God had truly blessed her beyond measure. The mother of four beautiful children, married to the man she had always loved, flawed in many ways, same as she. Yet this life was more than she could have ever imagined all those years ago in the grocery store. Esther smiled. God worked a small miracle through a bag of spilled Fruity Pebbles. *His ways are definitely not ours. That's a good thing, a very good thing.*

If you enjoyed this book, please take a few minutes to leave a review now. Authors, myself included, really appreciate this, and it helps draw more readers to books they may enjoy as well. Thanks! KC

Keep reading for a sample of Quinn and Ollie's story, Family Smarts and Runaway Hearts, coming the summer of 2023.

Sneak Peek

FAMILY SMARTS AND RUNAWAY HEARTS

"Red said you're leaving at the end of the week." Floyd stepped up to the food truck window, where Quinn Lewis waited for his sausage dog. The roar of the cement mixer several yards away in the soon to be parking lot hummed while George Jones blared from a nearby truck. "I'm supposed to talk you into staying until we finish everything." He glanced over his shoulder at the new three-story building that would soon be Red Goat, Alabama's first luxury hotel. "We'll be done in another month. What's your rush?"

Quinn Lewis reached through the window and took his sausage dog from the burly bald man in the off-white t-shirt with stained armpits and orange BBQ sauce splattered across his sizable chest. "Thanks Eric." Tattoos covered every part of the food truck owner's body from his chest to his wrists, but the big guy sure knew how to make a sausage dog. Quinn paid for his lunch, then turned to Floyd. "We've been cramped up in that little travel trailer together for six months. Nothing personal, but I'm pretty sick of you and I know you've got to be sick of me, too." He pulled the wax paper away from the soft steamy bun and took a bite. He glanced back at the food truck where the young woman in the hairnet and baggy t-shirt worked behind Eric. She kept her head down as she pulled the sausages from the warmer and put them in the steamed buns, then wrapped them in the flimsy papers. "It's time to get back to God's country."

"Awe man." Floyd spat a brown puddle of tobacco juice into the dust near Quinn's dusty steel toed work boots. "You are always out with a girl or some of the men when we're not working. We barely see each other, much less get on each other's nerves." He wiped the back of his hand across his mouth. "Think about all the money you're going to be leaving on the table if you go now."

"I can't help it." Quinn looked down at the man he had shared the tiny lodgings with ever since coming to town to work the construction job. "I miss my momma and the rest of my family. I've got to go."

"I sure do hate it." Floyd trailed along beside Quinn over to one of the rackety picnic tables where men from the work crew were sitting eating their lunch. "I'll have to pay your half of the rent until I can find somebody to take your spot. My wife won't like that. She is depending on the rent money I send her."

"Sorry man." Quinn threw one of his long legs over the wooden bench and straddled the seat. Floyd could spin a pitiful tale, but he wasn't fooling Quinn. He would have a new renter lined up for Quinn's end of the travel trailer before he drove off the lot on Friday.

Quinn watched Floyd walk away and took another bite of his lunch. He didn't have anything against the man, or the job, or the town, or even the state of Alabama. They were all fine, but they weren't Carson's Bayou. When he'd gotten laid off from the oil field last fall, he'd been thankful that he'd found a job with this crew. He was not in dire straits when it came to money, quite the opposite. For the past decade been investing most of his earnings and could have easily made it for a long, long time on his nest egg. When he was still out of work through Thanksgiving and then Christmas, however, he had to go to work or go stir crazy.

Now it was time to go home. He took a drink from his Gatorade bottle. The constant whirring of the cement mixer, the muffled chatter of different conversations, the music from the overzealous country music fan who shared his tunes from his enormous truck speakers with everyone there, gave the work site an almost festive vibe. This wasn't a bad job, and it definitely wasn't any harder than the offshore job he had before, but the truth of the matter was, Quinn was lonely. Sure, he went out on the weekends with some of the guys, and usually had a date with one of the ladies from the little town, but these people didn't know him, the real Quinn Lewis. The only people that truly understood him were his brothers, Drake and Hank. Even his momma didn't know him as well as she thought she did.

He shoved the last bite of the sausage dog into his mouth and wadded up the flimsy wax paper. A whistle blew across the yard and he stood up. Time to get back to work. He tossed his empty drink bottle and the paper in the trash barrel and strode across the dusty ground toward the building that would soon be completed. Sensing eyes upon him, he turned and looked across the yard to the food truck. The woman who had fixed his food met his eye. He smiled, and she turned her head away.

Was she Eric's wife, or possibly his sister? She was always there working, and always silent. She seemed lonely too, or was he just pushing his feeling off onto her? She was the only female on the site. What would make a woman choose that type of job? Tomorrow he'd speak to her, thank her for cooking his food. She probably didn't hear that often. These men were good enough folks, but most of them were a little rough around the edges. Not all of them. There were a few Bible thumpers like his brother Drake. One of those men may have thanked her for working the long days in the hot little truck for probably very little pay, but what if they hadn't? It didn't matter either way. She looked like a sad little gnome in her black hair net and baggy clothes. He could brighten her day before he left. He continued across the yard and headed back to work. Two more days, then he could get back home. Maybe then this longing for—something — would ease.

Ollie rolled the sausages over on the griddle, her mind wandering to other things. The steamy aroma of frying pork rose with the sizzle of the meat, unnoticed as it saturated her hair and clothing again today. Would she ever smell like something other than sausage? Her daddy said his stomach growled every time she walked in the room. She shifted her feet in the cramped workspace, careful not to bump into Eric standing in the window area, passing out the food and collecting the money.

When she had first fallen from grace and started working for the man, he had put her in the window serving the construction workers their food. That had lasted an entire thirty minutes before he demoted her to sausage flipper. When she handed a guy his lunch and he made the disgusting remark about sausages, she had reacted without thinking—her fist in his face. That was the story of her life, though, acting first and thinking later. Now she was working in a food truck, and not just in a food truck, in the back of a food truck where she couldn't screw things up.

At least Eric hadn't fired her that day. The louse with the bloody nose had gotten a free lunch. He'd also gotten a warning from Eric that if he harassed her again, the next punch would be from him and land the guy in the hospital. Eric could do it too, no doubt.

"Ollie look, let's remove temptation and let you flip for a few days," Eric had said, "until the men get used to a woman being in their midst."

"Temptation?" Ollie snorted, looking down at her grease stained t-shirt. "I'm sweating like a pig and this hair net is not exactly a fashion statement, Eric. That man was just being a jerk."

"Maybe so, but let's move you to the back. Most of these men are working away from home and don't see their wives and girlfriends for weeks on end. A lot of them don't know how to act around a lady, anyway." He wiped his gigantic hands on the dish towel tucked in his jeans. "I can't have you punching every guy in the face who comes on to you, or the foreman will have me run off the site."

"Come on to me?" Ollie wiped the back of her hand across her forehead. "He was being a horse's pa toot."

"That's the way idiots flirt, Ollie." The bear of a man grinned. "Here." He handed her the tongs. "You flip for a while. I'll run the window. Just to be safe." She had been the flipper ever since. It was for the best.

Her thoughts pulled back from her musings as the conversation at the window caught her attention. Quinn Lewis was leaving town? She dropped the sausage into the bun and took a step closer to where the men chatted. She wrapped the meat and bread in wax paper, careful to not draw attention to herself. She had been listening to all the workers every day, trying to pick out the best one to try her scheme on. So far, she had three candidates. Quinn Lewis, Donny West, and Andrew Norman, but if Quinn Lewis was leaving town on Friday, that put him as the top contender on her list.

The tall man with the scruffy beard and shaggy hair pulled

back in a ponytail wasn't much to look at, but that didn't matter. She wasn't in the looking business anymore, at least not in that way. She had studied the men for a long time and Quinn Lewis, along with the other two guys were from out of state, seemed to possess a few manners, and most importantly, had never given her a second glance.

Yeah, he would do. She would have to hustle to get everything ready by Friday, but she could make it work. She continued flipping sausage as the list of what needed to happen over the next couple of days solidified in her mind. She looked up as the lunch whistle blew, signaling the break was ending. Several men hurried to the counter to grab one more dog to wolf down before returning to work. She watched Quinn Lewis stroll away from the food truck toward the construction site, his stride long and self-assured, reminding her of Oscar, her oldest brother. Quinn turned suddenly, his chocolate eyes staring straight into hers. He smiled, and she tucked her head down. *Careful, don't draw attention to yourself now. Not when things are about to work out.*

"Ollie?"

Ollie blinked and looked up at Eric, staring down at her. "Hmmm?"

"I asked what's the sausage count? I've got to make a supply run this afternoon. Will the usual order get us through the rest of the week?"

"Uh." Ollie reached up and tucked a slim wisp of blond hair back in the hair net that clung to her head like an unwanted spider web, trapping her entire body in the life she longed to break free from. "Yeah, the normal order will do. Do you mind if I ride with you? I need to grab a couple of things before Owen picks me up this afternoon."

"Sure. I'll be going by your place. Why don't I just text your brother and tell him I'll drop you off? That way, you won't have to wait for him to pick you up."

"That would be awesome." She smiled up at the mountain of a man, one of the few true friends she had in this town. Would he still be her friend after Friday? "Eric, thank you—for everything."

"Sure thing." He bumped his beefy arm against her bony shoulder. "You know I couldn't make it without my Ollie behind me flipping and a stuffing."

Ollie looked away, shoving down the wave of guilt pushing up from her middle. She had to follow through with her plan. She had worked too long and too hard to back down now. Flipping and stuffing sausage dogs was not what she wanted to do for the rest of her life. She lifted her eyes back to the giant beside her. "Thanks, Eric."

"Anything for you, Ollie, you know that."

Read Family Smarts and Runaway Hearts

Join KC's newsletter and receive a free ebook of Music Smarts and Humble Hearts

Acknowledgments

Thank you to all the great readers who encourage me with your emails, contacting me on social media, and sending personal cards and notes. Your kind words mean so much to me. Of course, thank you for the reviews. Your kind words about my words plays an enormous part in others finding my work.

I am especially grateful for your prayers that sustain me as I craft my stories. I was under the weather for a bit while writing this one, but knowing you were lifting me up pushed me to write on.

Thank you to my wonderful ARC/Launch team. You ladies are a vital part of my writing ministry. Your willingness to come along beside me to get Christian Fiction into the hands of those who are searching is truly invaluable to me. You know who you are. Hugs to you, ladies.

Thank you, Mr. Wonderful. The list is too long, but you know what you mean to me.

Thank you, Lord for allowing me to serve You in this way. I never would have thought my big imagination and love of daydreaming could turn into a way to serve. I am blessed.

A Little About KC

KC sincerely believes that well-written Christian fiction can change lives. When a novel has strong Christian principals woven intricately into a well-written plot, the reader bonds with lifelike characters who struggle with trials, temptations, and struggles that the reader identifies with. The reader identifies with these characters because she's been there. Everyone has fallen. That's why everyone needs a Savior.

Then, when these same characters turn to Christ the Savior to bring them through these dark moments, the reader finds hope. KC believes the story reminds the reader why she must lean on the Lord in her trying situations. Through the book's structure showing Christianity as the positive light for good that KC knows to be true, the reader also sees why she needs to be the hands and feet of Christ to others.

KC strives to show how the Lord uses situations, people, and His Word to bring the lost to Him, and mold, prune and grow His children. She tackles challenging situations, powerful emotions, and spiritual warfare through engaging stories and true-to-life characters.

KC's favorite Bible verses are Philippians 2:5-8. Have this mind among yourselves, which is yours in Christ Jesus, who, though he was in the form of God, did not count equality with God a thing to be grasped, but made himself nothing, taking the form of a servant, being born in the likeness of men. And being found in human form, he humbled himself by becoming obedient to the point of death, even death on a cross.

KC cannot read these words without getting a lump in her throat. She strives daily to use her writing, her platform, her small influence to show others the love Christ has shown her.

If you enjoyed this book, please take a few minutes to leave a review now. Authors, myself included, really appreciate this, and it helps draw more readers to books they may enjoy as well. Thanks! KC

Join KC's newsletter and receive a free ebook of Music Smarts and Humble Hearts

Follow KC on her social media platforms

https://www.goodreads.com/author/show/20570083. K_C_Hart

https://www.bookbub.com/profile/kc-hart?list=author_books

www.amazon.com/author/kchartauthor

https://www.facebook.com/KCWRITESBOOKS

Books By KC Hart

A Christmas Blaze

Fresh Starts and Small Town Hearts

Business Smarts and Reckless Hearts

Car Smarts and Bashful Hearts

People Smarts and Wounded Hearts

Kid Smarts and Wistful Hearts

Family Smarts and Runaway Hearts

Elsie: Prairie Roses Collection

Moonlight, Murder and Small Town Secrets

Music, Murder and Small Town Romance

Memories. Murder and Small Town Money

Merry Murder and Small Town Santas

Medicine Murder and Small Town Scandal

Marriage, Murder & Small Town Schemes

Mistaken Murder & Small Town Status

Mistletoe, Murder & Small Town Scoundrels

Join KC's newsletter and receive a free ebook of Music Smarts and
Humble Hearts